I0747662

HELL HATH NO FURRY

HELL HATH NO FURRY
DIRTY DAISY MYSTERY SERIES
BOOK TWO

JORDYN KROSS

Scarlet Parlor Press LLC

This is a work of fiction. Names, characters, organizations, places, events, and incidents are either products of the author's imagination or are used fictitiously.

Copyright © 2022 by Jordyn Kross

All rights reserved.

No part of this book may be reproduced, or stored in a retrieval system, or transmitted in any form or by any electronic or mechanical means, including information storage and retrieval systems, without written permission from the author, except for the use of brief quotations in a book review.

Published by Scarlet Parlor Press, LLC

LCCN: 2022920257

Publisher's Cataloging-in-Publication

(Provided by Cassidy Cataloguing Services, Inc.).

Names: Kross, Jordyn, author.

Title: Hell hath no furry / Jordyn Kross.

Description: [Albuquerque, New Mexico] : Scarlet Parlor Press, LLC, [2022] | Series: Dirty Daisy mystery series ; book 2

Identifiers: ISBN: 978-1-7333808-9-8 (paperback) | 978-1-959691-00-6 (ebook)

Subjects: LCSH: Reporters and reporting--Texas--Fiction. | Weddings--Texas--Planning--Fiction. | Bridesmaids--Texas--Fiction. | Murder--Investigation--Fiction. | Man-woman relationships--Fiction. | LCGFT: Cozy mysteries. | Erotic fiction. | BISAC: FICTION / Romance / Erotic. | FICTION / Mystery & Detective / Cozy / General.

Classification: LCC: PS3611.R776 H45 2022 | DDC: 813/.6--dc23

Editor: Jenny Rardon

Cover: Brandi Doane McCann

ALSO BY JORDYN KROSS

Find all of Jordyn's books at jordynkross.com or here:

Melting Hearts Series
Prequel Novella - Jack's Frost
(free for newsletter subscribers)
Book 1 - Winter's List
Book 2 - Xmas Angel
Book 3 - Shattered Ice

The Yacht Club Series
Book 1 - The Handler
Book 2 - The Wrangler

Dirty Daisy Mystery Series
Book 1 - Dirty Daisy
Book 2 - Hell Hath No Furry

Uhraervi Brothers
Hung with Care
Open Enrollment

Pole Position

Fool's Gold

NOAH Series

Prequel Novella - Quantum Entanglements

Book 1 - Captain's Treasure

Book 2 - Stolen Fire

Nonfiction

Demystifying the Beats

Author Survival Guide

Single Titles

A Lost Claus

For my family, born to, married into, and found.

CHAPTER ONE

What did one wear to a spanking demonstration? Mikaela "Mike" Mitchell investigated her closet for the third time, shifting hangers with clever grammatical t-shirts and various shades of denim jeans. She glanced down at her current outfit. The glow-in-the-dark bat inviting people to the dark side was perfect October attire, but not for a seminar at the Tool Shed. The first event of the Daisy, Texas annual kink convention—Cowbells and Crops—required something a bit more serious.

If she didn't need information for her article, she'd stay home. Dressing up and hanging out with strangers was so not her thing. She tugged off her shirt, gritting her teeth. No pressure—just an entire town counting on her to make the convention sound spectacular in their revived paper, *The Daily Peat*. She snorted. More like a weekly newsletter that people paid to advertise in, but it was a paying job in her field and came with a living space. And even though she might be new to town, Daisy mattered to her, too.

With a sigh, she selected a plain black V-neck and black jeans. If she paired them with her flat black boots and silver earrings, she'd blend—with the BDSM crowd, at least. There was no blending with the furries that attended the event, unless she finally ordered that unicorn onesie she'd had saved in her Amazon account forever. And based on some of the elaborate gear the attendees had been dragging in with them to the inn, a onesie would get her laughed into the lake.

After quickly spreading on a fresh layer of deodorant, she donned her all-black camouflage. Then she tugged her long brown hair into a high ponytail and rushed out the door with a granola bar in one hand, cell in the other. The Tool Shed, a boutique sex-toy shop right behind the Flour Bed Bakery, was practically across the street from her home in the *Daily Peat* office.

Two steps onto the sidewalk, her phone rang—her bestie, the almost bridezilla. She answered, "Hey, Heather."

"Mike, I'm so glad I caught you. Did you get the topper?"

"Yep. Came in yesterday. Are you sure you want that on your wedding cake?" The antique topper, an enameled-wood bride and groom on a round metal platform, would likely survive an apocalypse.

"It's a Reinhardt tradition. One of his relatives made it before World War I."

"I'll make sure your baker gets it." Although it was a twenty-minute drive to the woman's house, Mike would find time somehow. At least Heather hadn't ordered from the Flour Bed. Mike could only imagine the pornographic outcome.

"Have you had a chance to see if the grounds can hold the larger tent? We got four more RSVPs today."

Shit. She'd completely spaced on her promise to walk the open field behind the Bloom with a View Inn, where her best friend was getting married next week. If she'd known the maid-of-honor assignment was going to be so intense, she'd have encouraged Heather and Jason to elope—too late to throw that out as an option. Instead, she scrambled for the answer that wouldn't put her friend deeper into a bridezilla frenzy. "I have an appointment in the morning. Janelle doesn't see any issues. But I'll take the measurements. No worries."

"Make sure the area where the tent will be is flat enough for the dance floor. I should have looked when I was out there, but I didn't think of it. I'm so sorry. I know you're busy, too. What's on today's agenda?"

"On my way to one of the convention demos so I have some fodder for the *Peat* posts." And sweating like a nun in a nudist colony because of the ridiculous October heat. Didn't Texas realize fall was supposed to be cool?

"There's a convention in town?" The panic in Heather's voice had Mike scrambling to calm her.

"Yep, but it's over on Sunday. Well before your guests will start to arrive."

"Whew. How's Ryder?"

Sexy as sin. Also annoying and overprotective. But gone for the moment. "He's good. Taking his cousin to the airport today."

"Aw. That man is such a sweetie. I swear he'd do anything for anyone. Tell him I said hi when you see him. Gotta run."

Heather wasn't wrong. She just didn't see the side of him that worried about everyone, too. Mostly he worried about imaginary dangers to Mike. And it was cramping her style. Well, maybe not *style*. She'd be the first to admit, she lacked style. But he was interfering with her job, which was so much worse. His words of concern still rang in her head: *You shouldn't go to that convention alone. There are a lot of good people, but it only takes one predator, and it's easier for them to blend into a costumed crowd.*

As if Mike wasn't a grown woman who could take care of herself. She'd proven it last summer when she'd helped him catch a killer.

A ping from a text broke into her internal rant. Speak of the sexy beast himself.

Ryder: *I'll be back tonight. Come over when you're done.*

Headline: Dominant Demon Demands Submissive Show Up

If only the articles came so easily. She snickered but didn't text it to him.

It was no surprise he wanted her to be at his place—the apartment over his mechanic's garage. The dependent side of her, the side she was trying to grow out of because it led to disappointment every time, heartily agreed. And granted, his six-foot muscular body fit in his bed much better than the tiny one at her place. But she loved her rooms that came with her job in the shotgun house that doubled as the *Daily Peat* office—especially the independence they represented. For the first time, she wasn't living with someone else, like her brother or Heather. Although if Mike's brother were still alive, she'd gladly move back in with him just to ease the constant ache of his absence.

Her brother's death had been what brought her to Daisy. It had been ruled a suicide, but there was no way he would do that—leave her voluntarily. She hadn't given up investigating, but she was no closer to the real story either. The only silver lining to the situation was meeting Ryder. He had been trying to get Mike to live with him practically a month after they started dating, but she refused. One day, she could totally see herself with Ryder in a cute little bungalow. But not so soon after they'd started dating, and *not* in the garage apartment.

At the door to the Tool Shed, Mike paused and typed a few letters into a text. A man in a cheetah outfit bumped into her while securing his cat head over sunlit blond hair. She rubbed her shoulder. Those furry heads were solid. With a quick glance, she realized there was no one else around. She checked the time. There were only seconds to spare before the afternoon demo started. She tucked her phone away, plastered on a smile, and entered the air-conditioned building to watch a grown woman—the town's deputy sheriff—get her ass spanked publicly by her lover.

CHAPTER TWO

RYDER RUIZ MERGED ONTO I-69 WITH HIS COUSIN BY HIS SIDE and his girlfriend miles away, alone at a BDSM convention. Although he'd insisted Mike go with them and then he would accompany her to the events the rest of the weekend, his arguments had zero impact on her stubbornness. Never mind that she'd been involved with a murder that summer and dumped on the side of the road by drug traffickers. Never mind he was still trying to figure out if her brother had really committed suicide or not, calling in all the favors he'd ever collected during his dark military missions. Never mind she was a walking accident looking for a place to happen. The woman had no sense of self-preservation. He protected her when she let him—which seemed to be less and less lately.

Donny cleared his throat, breaking the thorny silence in the cab of the truck. "I really appreciate you taking me to the airport."

"You're family. Not like I'm going to make you pay for a taxi or a shuttle from Daisy to Houston." Although with the six-hour round trip twice, once to drop Donny off and another to pick him up in ten weeks, his cousin probably could have driven to Virginia. But they were like brothers. Had grown up together after Ryder's parents ditched him with his grandparents. They even looked alike, aside from the six-inch height difference and the fact that Donny kept *his* dark hair trimmed regulation short. Ryder shouldn't be letting his concerns about Mike cloud his time with his cousin. "Class doesn't start until Monday. Why're you going early?"

"Never been. Want to see some things before it's full-on grind. After two and half months of training with the FBI, I'm not going to be in any shape to play tourist." Donny fidgeted with the crank for the passenger window.

"Did you ever figure out who in the county nominated you for this?"

"Never could get a straight answer. After all the trouble this summer with the illegal growers and the murders, I guess they figured they better develop my skills to hold down this corner of the county." Donny cracked a wry laugh.

Whoever had put his name in wasn't wrong. Summer had been a shit show, and although Donny was the sheriff, he didn't have a lot of experience with investigations. Ryder had helped out using his never-talked-about training, but that probably made the county boys even more nervous. Maybe they suspected, like Ryder, that they hadn't eliminated the drug problem, only scraped the surface.

"Of course," Donny drawled, "if all that hadn't happened, you'd have never met Mike."

Ryder grunted.

"She's good for you. I've never seen you so happy. When are you two going to move in together?"

"That's the thing." Ryder's relief at someone recognizing they should be cohabitating freed his tongue. "She won't consider living with me and will barely stay the night. That news office the county owns is on the main drag through town. She needs more security."

"Have you talked to the town council?"

"Of course. Weenie won't authorize any expense, not even for an alarm system, until the *Peat* is showing a profit. Mike's got more advertising lately, but it's still operating at a loss."

"You could just do it."

"Mike won't let me do any more other than the cameras. It's like she's not really committed to staying in Daisy, despite the job. Despite me asking her."

"Really?" Donny's shock reverberated over Ryder. "You asked her to marry you?"

"No." Ryder flashed his cousin a glare. "It's only been a few months." Not that he hadn't thought about it, but Mike would completely panic if he popped that question. "Just to live together, but she won't consider it. I sometimes wonder if she's going to bolt after Heather's wedding." Ryder wasn't sure what he'd do if that happened, but it would involve winning her back, because she'd embedded herself under his skin deeper than the tattoo over his heart.

Donny hummed his non-answer, and they rode quietly for several miles before he spoke again. "Do me a favor?"

"Anything." As if his cousin had to ask.

"Keep an eye on Berta Ann. If she needs anything, I told her she could ask you. Ten weeks is such a long time."

"Your deputy will be fine."

"I know. But with the convention in town, things can get a little crazy. I tried to delay it, but with only a few classes a year—"

"Nothing's gonna happen while you're gone, and the program's going to be epic. I'll be shocked if you stay in Daisy. You'll want to go someplace with real crime so you can use your new skills."

"No way. I love Daisy. Can't imagine living anywhere else." Donny sighed.

Ryder completely agreed. He'd be sent all over the world, but his heart remained in Daisy.

"The county's sending someone to fill in for me while I'm gone. Lance Kessler. Never worked with him. He's been with them over a year; we've just never met. I'm not sure how he's gonna get on with Berta Ann or the council. You know, being sheriff isn't all about just enforcing the laws. It's about keeping the peace."

"You do a great job."

Donny retrieved his phone from his carry-on. "I'll send you his contact info in case you need it. Berta Ann is having my patrol car detailed for him, and he's staying at my place. With the convention, nothing else was available."

Ryder's phone pinged with Donny's text a moment later, the sound only reinforcing the fact that Mike hadn't contacted him. He changed the topic to football and how Donny would miss Texas barbecue, anything that didn't require Ryder to pause from gnawing on what to do about Mike.

After dropping his cousin in the departures, Ryder exited the airport and stopped at the nearest fast-food joint. He used the restroom and bought a tea for the way home. Before leaving the parking lot, he sent a text to his buddy from his time in the military, Ike Parker, confirming he was still coming to the convention, and another message to Mike. By the time he made it to the freeway entrance, Ike had responded affirmatively—but it was clear his girlfriend wasn't going to answer. He turned up the radio. A popular cowboy was singing about sobbing into his adult beverage. Not a bad idea, except that Ryder was driving, Daisy was a dry town, and the Pink Petals strip club that straddled the state line was the last place he wanted to drown his relationship sorrows.

CHAPTER THREE

MIKE NAVIGATED HER WAY THROUGH THE TOOL SHED'S TIGHT retail space, done in lacquer white with jewelry store lighting. Every inch of the walls was used for displaying sex products, like leather crops, shelves of lube, and lingerie that consisted mostly of missing pieces. The scattered round tables held smaller toys, like clit stimulators, butt plugs, and cock rings according to the helpful signs. When Mike reached the door of the classroom, she hesitated.

Despite her all-black outfit, there was no way she could blend. In the far corner, Deputy Berta Ann Silva, her hair in pigtails, wore a coral tunic that showed off blindingly white bare legs. Her lover, Charlene "Chuck" Cooper, owner of the Love Me Knot Bait and Tackle, had dressed up for the occasion in clean blue jeans and a chambray shirt instead of her usual plaid. The adorable couple stood with their heads together in a private conversation.

Unwilling to interrupt, Mike took in the rest of the murmuring crowd. No one else was dressed as plainly as the couple kicking off the convention.

The vivid scene would be great for her article. She wasn't

allowed to take pictures, but she recorded it all in her head for later. The audience was packed with a mix of people in leather and metal, some attached to leashes, ironically not the ones in full furry costumes. All kinds of animals were represented in almost cartoonish quality, including a yellow bird seated next to a black-and-white cat, an orange-striped tiger, a white rabbit, a blue fox, and some kind of raptor. At the back of the room, a teddy bear stood next to a very large elephant.

The last time Mike had seen similar costumes, she'd been at a football game. Unlike the sports events, the quality of the conventioneers' outfits was on a completely different level. How did people discover they liked this? BDSM was out in the vanilla world, but furries? And how the heck did they end up at the same convention? As she inched around the room, it became clear she had a ton of research to do.

The tiger shifted, and Letty, the middle-aged owner of the Flour Bed Bakery, in her signature leopard-print leggings, was leaning into the cat, fingering his fur, likely trying to sink her claws into him. Although the scene had an intimate quality, Letty wasn't smiling her usual flirty smile. What was the story there?

Mike stopped staring. She was being unfair—she had no idea what they were saying. Although Letty spent so much time hitting on Ryder, Mike couldn't help being a bit catty. An array of appetizers just beyond the couple called to her, including the Flour Bed's famous maple bars with their bonus donut holes. They always looked far too phallic for it to be unintentional. After the demo, she'd dig in.

The room had few empty chairs. Mike spotted two, one in the back next to a woman dressed head-to-toe in faux-leather with a full feathered face mask, her hair knotted in a tight bun, and her spine ramrod straight. The other free seat was next to Olive Hardins, the headliner and owner of the Pink Petals strip club. Mike moved to her aisle. Olive wore an amazing red leather dress and matching thigh-high boots with a heel that could perform surgery. She flashed a quick crimson-lipped smile as Mike sat. A niggle of guilt crawled up her neck as she dug into her satchel to retrieve her notebook and pen. She'd accused the woman of murder last summer. Fortunately, Olive hadn't held a grudge, and the fact that *she* had bothered to attend the demo meant it would be article worthy.

No sooner had Mike settled in when another Domme, dressed in skinny leather pants with lacing up the front, a sweetheart bustier, and Victorian-style boots, stepped up to the front of the room. She inspected the crowd. Silence descended with her weighty presence. Tiger dropped into the chair Mike had avoided, while Letty remained with her risqué donut display.

The Domme's voice rang out crisp and clear, "Thank you all for attending this afternoon's educational session. Thank you to the Tool Shed and Violet Savage for hosting the Cowbells and Crops seminars once again. Violet was sorry she couldn't join us today, but she sends her kind regards. Thanks to our sponsors, the Flour Bed Bakery and...Bay Leaves restaurant, for the lovely spread. But now, the reason we're all here. I'm so pleased to present Chuck and her partner, Berty. They will provide the impact play demonstration for us. Please give them the respect they deserve and save your questions for the end."

Mike shifted in her chair as a shiver of anticipation passed through her.

Chuck came to the forefront. "Hi everyone. Glad you could make it today for the first demo of the conference. It's great to see so many of you decked out for the event already." She waited for the applause and animal calls to subside. "This demonstration is going to cover the basics of impact play. Communication, warm-up, proper placement, and aftercare. I'll be explaining as I go, but please hold your questions until the end."

She settled onto a hardback armless chair and held out her

hand to Berta Ann, or Berty, as she was being called for the demo. Berty walked to her partner in bare feet and paused, her side to the audience and her face turned to Chuck. Low words were exchanged. Chuck grazed her fingers down Berta Ann's arm slowly.

Chuck shifted her focus to the audience. "I've just reviewed our parameters for this scene and confirmed her safe word. This is not for punishment but for education and, secondarily, pleasure. At any point, Berty can stop this with a word. Berty, remove your panties."

Oh holy crap. Mike hadn't expected the deputy to be baring it all or at least not the important parts. But Berty, head high, reached under the tunic and slipped her simple briefs down her legs. Chuck clasped her free hand and assisted her with stepping out of them then picked up the discarded cotton and tucked them in her jeans. Berty smiled at Chuck, who patted her lap. Down went Berty, baring her ass when the tunic shifted, and she draped herself over Chuck's knees. Mike leaned back in her chair and pressed her knees together. She had to give it to the deputy—there was no way Mike could do something like that in front of strangers or, more importantly, in front of people she knew. Berta Ann, as the deputy sheriff, knew everyone.

Chuck rested one hand on Berty's lower back, while the other moved in slow circles around Berty's narrow, perfect bum. Maybe if Mike's ass were that nice, she wouldn't be scared to share it. As Chuck continued to stroke her lover's back, her bare skin, a bubble formed around them. The silence of the audience filled the room until Mike imagined she could hear the soft strokes of skin on skin.

Chuck lifted her hand and smacked down on Berty's right cheek. The sound stung Mike's ears.

Ouch.

Maybe not.

Ryder gave Mike's ass the occasional smack during sex, but that was on a different level. And private.

The smacks continued, increasing in intensity as Chuck occasionally commented about spanking techniques and warm up and placement. She never let her gaze stray from the lover on her lap.

Mike resisted the urge to squirm. She glanced at Olive, who gave her another sly half smile, a look that only added to Mike's unease. It was only the first day of the Cowbells and Crops convention, and this was only her first event. Mike wasn't sure how she would get through attending everything, much less write it up later.

Chuck stopped spanking and held up a brown tube about a foot long, her fingers barely meeting around the girth. Her other hand still held Berty in place on her lap.

It looked like a giant leather dildo.

Chuck dragged it up Berty's inner leg and over the seam of her ass before repeating the same move with the other leg. Berty squirmed the tiniest bit, and Chuck thumped the dildo across Berty's already pink cheeks. She kept a rhythmic pace, and Berty's flesh rippled with the impact. The spanking continued for several more minutes, Berty's skin getting redder and redder. She began to shake and shift. A soft sound, half whimper and half moan, rose above the thud of the impact.

Mike shifted in her chair. The room had shrunk and was much warmer than before the demo started.

Finally, Chuck stopped, rested the dildo along Berty's back, and proceeded to rub her sub's abused butt while whispering to her. Berty turned her head toward Chuck, but Mike couldn't tell if she spoke or not.

After a moment, Chuck refocused on the audience and asked for questions. The silence broke with an audible gasp. Hands and paws shot up.

Mike released the breath she'd been unconsciously holding,

jotted down some of the more interesting questions, and made some additional notes about the overall experience. The intimacy Chuck and Berta Ann had achieved even in a crowd shocked Mike. It didn't seem possible, but she'd witnessed it along with about thirty other people. Were they as aroused as she was? And just as discomfited?

"If you'd like to see this up close," Chuck said, holding the dildo aloft, "you're welcome to. Just give me a few minutes first." She then placed it to the side of the chair and guided Berta Ann off her lap. Chuck embraced Berta Ann in a tight hug and peppered kisses all over her face, murmuring to her and petting her hair. She escorted Berta Ann to the side, where a padded bench had been placed, and assisted her in sitting, covering her with a small lap blanket and handing her an open bottle of water. She stood by as Berta Ann took a couple of sips.

Back at the demonstration chair, Chuck held up the tool and waved people over. Some went back to the pastries. Some were already leaving. Mike worked her way to the front so she could capture the details about the instrument for her story. The conference barred photos at the demos, so she had to get as many notes down as possible. As she waited in line for her turn, someone pressed against her. She turned but was met with a face full of orange-striped fur.

"Did you like the spanking?"

In five words, the stranger skeeved Mike out. His tone was laced with innuendo and mastery. As if. She stepped back hard, right on the tiger's paw. The sound that came out of the furry head wasn't tiger-like at all.

"I'm so sorry. I didn't realize you were right behind me." She blinked up at the mesh space.

He growled at her, but the line had freed up, and Mike left the asshole to talk to Chuck.

"That was a great demo."

Berta Ann rejoined her lover, giving Mike a shy smile.

"Would you mind telling me more about the, uh..." Mike wiggled her index finger at the tool in Chuck's hand.

"Sure." Chuck held out the dildo, and Mike took it. Her hand dropped from the unexpected weight of the deceptively plain brown tube. "The leather is hand-sewn, and the sand provides a nice thuddy experience."

"Wow, that could really leave a mark." The leather was warm, and the sand tightly filled the tube.

"It has," Berta Ann replied with a laugh.

"But it didn't seem like you were in much pain." Mike had been keeping an eye out for signs of distress on Berta Ann's part. "In fact, I thought you were enjoying it."

"Never been spanked by a lover?"

Ugh, that voice. Tiger was back. Mike ignored the creepy furry and handed the dildo back to Chuck.

"This was just for fun and the demo." Berta Ann laughed and nudged her shoulder into Chuck's arm. "Chuck can wield that with a lot more power when she wants to."

Chuck grinned and stepped away, waving the irritating tiger over to her.

"What about the audience?" Mike asked Berta Ann. "Were you comfortable with the exhibitionism, especially with your role in the community?"

"Being submissive isn't something I'm embarrassed about. It doesn't change who I am at my day job. The people here who know me respect me not only for the job I do, but also for the submission I give Chuck. They understand the strength it takes to let go."

"I want to do an article on this for *The Daily Peat*. Would it be okay if I quote you? Or I can keep it anonymous."

"Leave the last names and my job title out. Otherwise, go for it." Berta Ann stood tall in her bare feet.

Mike nodded. "Of course."

A thud on the table as Chuck slammed her hand down made Mike jump.

"It's time for you to go," Chuck said as she grabbed the arm of the tiger man and escorted him out of the building.

"Damn it." The Domme who'd opened the demonstration trotted by, chasing Chuck.

Mike and Berta Ann shared a wide-eyed glance before Mike tucked away her notebook. "I'm going to get something to eat before I go. Do you want anything?"

"No. But thanks for coming and for the interview," Berta Ann said before turning her attention to the next person in line.

Mike rushed to the back of the room, hoping there was some food left and that Letty was gone. Her stuff might look obscene, but it was tasty. And Mike was starving.

Jackpot.

Not only were there Flour Bed treats, but also some Boudin balls from Bay Leaves. Mike popped one into her mouth, the sausage deliciously spicy. She grabbed three more before searching for a plate or napkin.

A deep laugh startled Mike, and she scrambled to not drop her goods.

"I see you found my balls." The Cajun accent rolled over her in a soothing wave.

"Hey, Tank. If I'd known you were catering, I'd have come over earlier. There's not much left."

"You come to the restaurant anytime, cher. I'll feed you up."

Mike laughed at the gentle redheaded giant. She'd be in his restaurant every day if she could afford his prices. "Are you catering the dance contest tonight?"

"No. I don't know what Valerie organized for that one."

"Darn." A girl could hope.

"The only reason I got *this* gig is that Ms. Savage was coordinating it."

"I haven't met her. Is she here?" Mike had only lived in Daisy for a few months, but she'd never even heard Violet Savages's name before tonight.

"What are *you* doing here?" An acerbic and recognizable voice emanated from the feather-masked Domme. The same one Mike had avoided earlier.

"Hi, Weenie." Mike smiled at the town council chair, despite the harsh tone. "Nice to...well, I can't say that I can see you. How are you? Enjoy the spanking?" She walked a fine line, since technically Edwina "Weenie" Alman was her employer.

"You're planning on putting this in our paper? We said no pictures."

The woman had a say in her employment, but not in what she wrote. Not as long as Mike held the job. "Didn't take any. But people come here every year for the BDSM and furry convention. I think it'll be a big attention getter. Unless there's another event that I'm missing?"

"The BDSM and Furry communities don't typically mix. This is a unique pairing that has worked for several years. I don't want to risk offending either side or our town getting a bad reputation."

"You mean like for trafficking drugs or something? I can't imagine reporting on this demo would lead to negative attention like that. I mean the motto 'Safe, Sane, Consensual' sort of implies sober." Mike was going to get in trouble if she didn't bite her tongue instead of hinting at the events of last summer and Weenie's late husband's involvement.

"There is a giant chasm between sober and appropriate for the paper."

"Don't worry. I'm a professional." Mike waved as she sped away, rushing back to her office. It was damn unnerving talking to a person whose face was covered with feathers and body wrapped in faux-leather about propriety.

After typing out her notes for the article, there was barely any time to get ready for the dance competition. Mike glanced down at herself. No reason to change. It wasn't like she had something better to wear. She microwaved a box dinner, scarfing it down. A quick freshen up of her hair and makeup, and she was on her way, locking the office as she left. The community center was practically next door to the newspaper.

Mike glanced at her phone. Ryder's unanswered text from earlier niggled her conscience. Nope, no time. She tucked the phone into her back pocket and stayed on course, excited to find out what the Cowbells and Crops Dance Competition entailed.

The air had finally started to cool now that the sun had set. The asphalt parking lot was filled with cars and latecomers, several dressed in street clothes with an occasional tail, headed to the single-story cream painted–cinderblock building. There'd never been so many people at the center since she'd moved to Daisy. The sounds of booming EDM met her at the metal double doors. She yanked one open and halted before she ran into Caleb, her favorite book-nerd bouncer.

"What are you doing here?" she yelled over the music. He should be at the Pink Petals, but it was nice to see a familiar face.

"Checking IDs. Eighteen and over. Bar's closed until after the show."

Mike nodded and reached for her driver's license in her back pocket, but Caleb waved her off.

Spotlights danced over the hordes of people, most of them clad in leather and synthetic fur. They clustered around a stage lit with professionally hung canned lighting. The dancers on stage pantomimed an orgy in time to the booming bass DJ Slick spun from the far corner. With a deep breath, Mike let the door close behind her and sidled around the edge of the room. Slick, the skinny blond man she'd met that summer, waved her over.

"Aren't you working?" Mike asked.

"It's taped." He sat back on a stool and propped one foot up. "Where's Ryder?"

"Had to do a favor for his cousin. Besides, *I'm* working."

"Yeah? Be sure to mention me in the article." He gave her a cheesy grin.

"I will if you can get some of the acts to talk to me."

"Too easy." He stood and pointed to the edge of the black satin curtains. "Behind there is the 'backstage.'" He wiggled his fingers in air quotes. "They're all changing and practicing."

"Thanks." Mike left him as the music wound down and the group ended their performance in a complex pyramid that would never be allowed in a cheerleading competition. That group had to have serious trust, based on the locations of feet, faces, and crotches.

"Give it up for Pant-o-Mimes," Slick bellowed into his mic, reading from a preprinted paper. "Next up, we have Rainbow Star in a solo performance."

A woman clad in colorful body paint, glitter, hooves, a gold horn on a headband, and a horsey tail that was anchored in a way Mike didn't want to imagine, entered the stage. It was like the woman was wearing the onesie Mike had saved but without the fabric. The opening notes of an eighties pop song kicked off her happy prancing around the stage.

Mike slipped behind the curtain, trying to be ready for anything but hesitant to look around. The scene backstage could have been the fodder for a cult flick. People in various states of dress or undress applied makeup or moved through shallow imitations of their routine. Mike approached a group of furries that didn't seem to be busy, but before she reached them, the elephant pushed the tiger—the same creep from the spanking demo—making him stumble. The tiger tore off his head. His dark hair with blond highlights mimicked his costume. He reached for the elephant before the bear stepped in. Mike couldn't hear what the bear said, but the tiger wasn't muffled.

"I'm not doing the stupid group routine. It's the same dumb plan as last year. I'm soloing."

Mike ambled closer, pretending not to eavesdrop.

"You should have told us earlier, dude," the bear said.

"I'm fucking done with you, asshole," the elephant shouted. "Fuck off and die. Don't ever call me again." The elephant turned his back, and a Domme who had been standing too close jumped back to avoid being hit by his trunk. "He's your fucking problem, now," he told the woman before stomping off.

"Jackass," the tiger mumbled. He set his head on the nearby table and then opened his fur suit with the telltale rip of Velcro, freeing the top from the pants. Whoever had made the suit was a genius, because Mike would have never guessed it came apart like that. He dropped the top over a folding chair and picked up a small bottle.

"I told you this was a mistake," the Domme said to him, crossing her arms and tapping her foot. She was the same woman who'd introduced the spanking demo. "You should've listened to me."

"Stick to being bossy in the bedroom, babe. You don't understand my vision, and I don't need you managing my life." The tiger was rubbing his exposed skin with oil from the bottle. He snapped it closed and wiped his hands carefully on a towel before slipping on his paw mittens and putting on his head.

Dude was an ass, but he was a half-naked tiger, and the naked part wasn't bad.

"You're going to regret this," the Domme said before spinning on her spiked heel and strutting away.

Mike shivered. The woman was scary pissed, and Mike wasn't even the object of her wrath.

"Thank you, Rainbow Star," DJ Slick's voice rang out. "And

now, a surprise addition to the line-up, please welcome Tiger Beat."

The tiger tucked through the center opening in the curtain where the sparkly unicorn had just come through. The song started. Of course. Mike barked out a tight laugh. She was certain Tiger Beat would be "beating it" by himself in the near future unless he let the dominating woman beat him as punishment.

Glancing around, the rest of the acts seemed occupied, and Mike didn't want to intrude. She returned to the safety of the DJ stand. The tiger was surprisingly talented. He actually had a routine that worked. It could be extremely difficult to be seductive on stage based on her one stint at being a stripper. Of course, he wasn't dancing in stacked stilettos. Cat calls and whistles filled the air as he finished his performance.

"He's got it in the bag," Slick said.

"There's a prize?"

"First prize is five hundred." He handed her a flyer that showed the best group and the best solo each had prize money for the top three acts. No wonder his buddies were pissed.

CHAPTER FOUR

THE NEXT DAY, LATE FOR HER MORNING APPOINTMENT, MIKE hurried to the Bloom with a View Inn. She parked by the green and gold Bay Leaves sign and raced around the connected buildings. Darting across the wide porch with the matching white rockers, she yanked open the inn's bluebonnet-blue front door. Janelle stood behind the shabby-chic dresser turned front desk, chuckling as Mike tripped inside, clinging to the doorknob to avoid a face plant.

"Girl. You're gonna hurt yourself one of these days."

Mike regained her balance and closed the door to the cozy lobby outfitted in chalk-painted, chintz-covered furniture and a few antique doilies. "I didn't want to be late."

"Don't rush on my account. I'm not going anywhere." Her smile rose to her warm brown eyes. The slender woman was always so put together, with her close-cropped curls and a crisp white blouse with an embroidered collar. "Now, the important question. Have you eaten?"

"Did Ryder tell you to ask that?" Mike's cheeks heated. The man was forever asking people to look out for her.

"Tank has breakfast waiting for us. Come on."

Mike followed the woman through the ground floor of the inn, never getting tired of the white beadboard walls accented with bluebonnet-blue and lavender. Even the artwork, Texas landscapes, stayed on theme. The aroma of coffee and bacon strengthened with every step toward the restaurant. Janelle didn't wait for a server, just guided them to a two-seater table in the glass-enclosed area that looked over the marina.

The redheaded Cajun chef placed two coffees in front of them the moment they were seated.

"Thank you, Tank." Janelle smiled up at the giant of a man whose hand rested on the back of her chair.

"My pleasure." Tank's voice held a note of warmth Mike never heard him use except with Janelle. "What brings you here, today, Mike? Besides my stuffed French toast."

Mike's stomach rumbled in appreciation. She could almost taste the toasted pecans Tank sprinkled over the custard and berry–filled bread. "I promised Heather I would walk the grounds where the tent is going for the reception next week."

"Walk the grounds?" he scoffed. "There's no need for that. We have tents here all the time."

"I know, but I promised."

"These brides today." Janelle shook her head, her warm brown eyes sparkling.

"You shouldn't go alone. Last thing I need is you twisting your ankle out there all by yourself." Tank crossed his arms. "And I've got lunch to prep. Maybe you can come back this afternoon, and I'll go with you."

Her lack of grace was well-known, but this was walking—no high-heels involved. "I'm just going to pace off the space. I'm wearing my high-tops." She held out her foot to prove her point. "Besides, it will help me work off your delicious meal. And I'll be quick. I have to get to some of the conference events today so I can write them up for the *Peat*."

"Tank," Janelle said, "Mike'll be fine." She reached up and patted his arm, her dark skin in contrast to his pale freckles.

Tank softened immediately at her touch, dropping his arms and emitting a low grumble before he left.

"That man." Janelle's gaze hadn't left the retreating chef. "So protective."

Mike bit back the personal question she was dying to ask, because if Janelle and Tank had something going on, no way would she tell Mike. Instead, they reviewed the room count for Heather's wedding, the timing of the ceremony, and the plans for the delivery of the tent, tables, and chairs. Tank would provide the food, but Janelle was in charge of everything else. As they'd discussed at least three times before. But that was what maids of honor did for their bestie brides. At least the breakfast was amazing and free.

"All right. You go do your walk around, and let me know if you see anything that might be a problem." Janelle patted Mike's shoulder and returned to the lobby.

Mike slurped the last of the rich chicory coffee and escaped out the back door of the restaurant.

Lush green grass filled the space between the white-painted clapboard Victorian and a dense hardwood forest, framing the far edge of the field. To the right, in the distance, the curved road hugged the lawn. To her left, past the restaurant's gravel lot, the view of the marina and lake only added to the sense she inhabited a picture postcard. Exactly why she'd convinced Heather to have her wedding at The Bloom.

Mike paced across the lawn, counting her strides. An event decorator she'd interviewed back in Houston when she still worked for the community paper shared the improvised yard-stick trick. She counted to twenty-five before she was at the edge of the forest. The leaves were still vibrantly green, and the shade provided a welcome retreat from the heat already building in the cloudless blue sky. As Mike walked in a few more feet, turning to check out the view from this new perspective, a flash of orange caught her eye.

She took a few steps farther, in between the trunks of the leafy trees. The furry tiger from the night before was lying directly on the ground, curled slightly. The top of his costume covered the carved abs he'd displayed the night before in the dance competition. Had he had too much to drink and passed out?

Mike couldn't leave him there. She moved in and nudged him with her high-top. Nothing. She bent down and shook him by the shoulder. "Hey, Tiger. Wake up."

His body shifted, and the tiger head rolled.

Mike jumped back. A scream froze on her lips. She'd only seen him with his furry head or from the back and had no idea what he looked like. And she never would. At least not as he'd once looked. But that was the same blond-streaked hair she'd seen last night, framing what remained of his face. Raw meat had more shape. Her breakfast rose in her throat.

Tiger was dead—definitely dead. Someone had beaten the man to death.

Mike glanced around the body. Trails of sand covered the loamy forest earth. They were too far from the lake's shore—it didn't make sense.

Headline: Big Cat Beached by Forest Beat Down

Mike shivered and backed out of the forest to the edge of the grass. She had to call someone. She pulled her phone from her pocket and dialed the only person she wanted to talk to in that moment.

"'Bout time you called me back." Ryder's voice, even irritated, soothed Mike's panic.

"Something bad happened."

"Are you okay?" His tone shifted to concern.

"I am. But—"

"Where are you, M?"

Mike took a breath. "The inn—near the forest in their south forty."

"What happened?"

"There's a dead tiger. I mean a guy, dressed as a tiger. But he's dead."

"Are you safe?"

That was a good question. Mike glanced around. "Yeah, no one's here but me and the dead guy."

"Don't touch anything. I'm on my way."

Mike ended the call but itched to run rather than stand in a field alone with a dead body. What was wrong with this town? For the second time, she found herself drawn into a murder. At least she didn't know the victim this time. Not really. Not even his full name. But based on what little she did know, it wasn't that surprising someone had it in for him. She strained to recall the details from the events of the previous night. Could the elephant have been mad enough to do this? Or was it—

Movement near the road caught Mike's eye. Ryder. He strode toward her on long jean-clad legs ending in motorcycle boots. Dark-brown hair flowed loosely behind him, and his white t-shirt hugged his chest. She could use a hug, too. His gaze locked on her, and she ran across the field to meet him.

He enveloped her in his strong embrace. "You're okay. I got you."

The words rumbled through her, allowing her to take a breath. Her first since she'd found the body. She pressed back so she could see his warm brown eyes. "It's awful."

"Show me."

She took his hand and led him to the murder. Ryder released her and prowled around the body from a distance. "Did you touch anything?"

"I nudged him with my foot. Maybe his shoulder? I thought he was passed out drunk. His head rolled off and then—" Mike swallowed hard.

He pointed at a bloody rag and glanced up.

"I didn't notice that. Only the sand."

Ryder nodded. "Anything else?"

"Yeah. He was at the spanking demo. Chuck had to kick him out."

"Why?"

"I'm not sure. Something he said, I guess. He was at the dance competition last night, too." She filled Ryder in on what she'd seen backstage.

"I called Berta Ann already." Ryder tugged his phone from his pocket and touched the screen. "She'll bring the officer covering for Donny, but it's gonna be a little while. She's just getting back to town with Donny's patrol car. You gonna be alright? Want to wait with Janelle?"

Mike shook her head. "Should I call Heather? This could ruin her wedding. And I talked her into having it here. Crime scene investigators tramping by the tent wasn't exactly what I'd planned for the reception. I know I should be more upset about the dead guy, but—"

Ryder held up a hand. "Don't call Heather. You'll only upset her. I'm sure the officer filling in for Donny will be able to get this resolved. Based on the wounds, it's likely a crime of passion, not premeditation. I'm sure it will wrap up quickly and she won't even know."

CHAPTER FIVE

RYDER HELD MIKE IN HIS ARMS. SHE SHIVERED, EVEN THOUGH IT had to be past eighty degrees already.

She checked her watch for the millionth time. "When will they be here?"

"You should stay with me for the rest of the convention. Or at least until they find the killer."

"This can't drag on." She wrenched herself from his hold.

His emptied embrace stung. "It won't. I'll make sure of it. But—"

"I'll help."

"No." This woman was going to be the death of him. "You are not going to involve yourself in another murder."

"Oh, but you are? You don't even know who this guy is. I know all kinds of things about him. And I was there when he was pissing people off." She narrowed her eyes at him. "Besides, you know I'm good at getting information. You need me."

He did, but not to investigate a murder. That's why they had a loaner officer. So he and Mike could be civilians.

"I'm already covering the convention. If I happen to find out something helpful…" She shrugged.

Ryder scrubbed a hand over his face.

"Hey, Ryder." Berta Ann's voice rung out from a couple yards away. "This is Officer Lance Kessler."

Ryder spun around. He'd been so distracted with Mike, he hadn't keyed on them coming up behind him. He held out his hand. "Ryder Ruiz. Nice to meet you. Sorry it's under these circumstances."

"Didn't expect to catch a case on arrival." The guy looked like a California surfer. Lean, blond, and uniform just a bit too tight. Trendy aviators hid his eyes.

"This is Mikaela Mitchell." Ryder placed his hand on Mike's back. "She found the body."

"Ma'am." The officer tipped his head, his gaze lingering a moment too long.

Mike leaned forward. "You look like someone—"

"Can you show me?" Officer Kessler cocked his head toward the crime scene.

Ryder blocked Mike's path. "I can show him. No need for you to see that again."

"I'll stay with her," Berta Ann said.

Mike frowned but didn't move. Finally, she complied with one instruction. Ryder led the loaner cop to the costume-clad corpse.

"One of the conventioneers, then."

Ryder nodded. "Seems so."

"Don't guess he's got a wallet on him." The officer started taking pictures with his cell phone.

"If he does, it's under the costume."

"We'll wait for the crime scene team, then. Did you notice this sand and this?" Kessler pointed to the bloody rag.

"Looks like leather. Sand's embedded in the grain."

"Huh? Sand-filled leather. Would take a pretty big person to crush someone's face with something like that I imagine."

"Strong at least." Ryder leaned toward it being a man, but he'd known some women capable of the crime.

"Vic's pretty tall." Kessler snapped another image.

"Could have been kneeling. Did you see the leaves and dirt?" There were stains on the tiger's knees.

"Or he could have fallen after the first blow. Maybe from behind?" The officer paced around again. "No footprints."

"Hasn't rained in quite a while."

"He couldn't have been wearing the headgear when he was attacked."

"True." Not particularly useful, but true.

"Let's go talk to Mikaela."

"She goes by Mike. And full disclosure, she's my girlfriend and a reporter." Who wasn't going to keep her nose out of this no matter how Ryder protested.

Kessler turned his back and ambled out of the woods. "So, Mike?"

She faced the officer, but her gaze was on Ryder. She still looked a bit rattled from her discovery. He gave her what he hoped was a reassuring nod.

"How did you come to be out here on a Friday morning just in time to find a body? Doesn't look like this area gets much foot traffic. Did you see the body from the field?"

"No, not until I was practically on top of him." Mike explained about Heather's wedding and her need to have a flat space for her tent and the dance floor.

"I'm going to check the scene." Berta Ann walked toward the forest.

Kessler nodded and addressed Mike. "Did you know the victim?"

"Not really. I mean, I don't know his name."

"Tell me what you do know." Kessler pulled out a notebook and jotted notes periodically as Mike explained her interactions with the dead furry. Ryder tried to read over Kessler's shoulder, but it looked like he was using a personalized shorthand.

"That's all I know." Mike glanced at the inn. "But I'm going to be at the convention for my paper. If I find out anything more, I can let you know."

Kessler puffed up. "I'm not sure—"

"I'll be attending with her." Ryder moved to stand next to Mike.

"Well, in that case... I mean, with your skills..."

What the hell did this guy think he knew?

Kessler continued, tone reverent, "You're kind of a legend, especially with how you helped Sheriff Ruiz last summer."

Ryder was going to speak to his cousin about gossiping.

Mike's forehead wrinkled, and she opened her mouth. Ryder turned to avoid whatever she had to say. It could wait until they didn't have an audience.

Berta Ann, pale with a slight wobble to her step, emerged from the trees. It was a gruesome scene, especially for Daisy.

Kessler indicated to the air behind them. A white van had parked on the road next to Ryder's motorcycle. That was the fastest the crime scene unit had ever arrived in Daisy.

"We have to tell Janelle and Tank." Mike tugged Ryder's hand.

"I don't think—" Ryder barely got the words out before Kessler cut him off.

"Let's try to keep this quiet. Don't want hysteria with all these visitors. And we don't have a positive ID. I'd prefer to notify the next of kin before they hear it through the grapevine."

"It's not like a body bag being wheeled across the lawn and a bunch of people running through the woods is going to go unnoticed," Mike argued, not at all quelled by the officer's imperious tone. "We have to tell the owners something. Plus, there's a lot of people from the convention staying here. They might know something about Tiger Beat and who would want to kill him."

"Tiger Beat?" Ryder asked.

"Uh, yeah. I started calling him that in my head after his dance performance."

"We'll get to that, ma'am." Kessler crossed his arms. "But we need time to deal with the body before we start questioning everyone who might know something."

Berta Ann stepped between Mike and Kessler. "Mike and Ryder know how to be discreet. Let's you and me deal with the body and see about the identification."

She led the visiting officer away from the scene, and Ryder followed Mike across the field.

Ryder held the door to the inn open for Mike.

Janelle emerged from the guest hallway, eyes glued to her phone. She tucked it away when she noticed them. "Ryder, what's going on? Mike, everything okay with the lawn?"

"The lawn is fine, but there's kind of another problem." Mike glanced up to Ryder.

"Is Tank here?" Ryder asked.

Janelle nodded. "In the kitchen. He's catering the Cowbells' fashion show today. I was just tidying some rooms. One of my girls called in."

"I think this is worth an interruption, and if we tell you both at the same time, it would be better." Ryder indicated she should lead the way.

Janelle glanced back at Ryder and Mike as she strode down the hall. "Don't tell me the gophers are back."

"No," Mike answered. "It was something a little bigger than that."

"Let's wait until we get to the kitchen." Ryder wasn't sure who were in the rooms they were passing and what might be overheard.

"Tank?" Janelle called out. "Ryder's here. He needs to talk with us."

"One second," the chef answered as he slid a tray of pralines from the oven onto a cooling rack. "Last one." He wiped his hands on the towel he'd used to remove the tray and then flipped the fabric over his shoulder.

No point in sugarcoating the situation. "Mike found a body. Out in the woods."

Janelle gasped her hand going to her throat.

"Who?" Tank asked.

"One of the convention attendees. Don't know much at this point, but there's likely to be some investigation activity going on. Just wanted to give you a heads-up."

"I'm sorry about your guests having to see all that," Mike told Janelle.

"I doubt many of them will see much. The place emptied out about an hour ago. Everyone went to the community center for the fashion show. You have to get there early to get a good seat. Standing room only, I was told."

"Any guests missing that you noticed?" Ryder asked.

"No. At least I don't think so, but I guess they'll have to question everyone?"

"Officer Kessler and Deputy Silva will handle the investigation." Ryder gave Mike a pointed look. "We're only here to let you know about the situation—"

"But anything you know would help," Mike added, once again ignoring his signals.

"We had a full house for breakfast." Tank shifted closer to Janelle. "Mike got here just after everyone left. I fixed her and Janelle some breakfast and then got started doing the final prep for the catering. Speaking of which…" Tank glanced at a clock hanging over the door to the kitchen. "I need to get this food packed up."

"We can help." Mike nudged Ryder.

He gave a quick nod to Tank's questioning glance. "We're going to the center."

"*You're* going to the convention?" Janelle's teasing tone brought back the memories of the disaster that had been Ryder's first and last Cowbells and Crops convention. "I thought you swore them off after the first one."

"Mike convinced me."

"What?" Mike whipped around to glare at him.

"She has to get her articles for the paper, but she doesn't want to put herself at risk when there's a killer in town." Ryder raised an eyebrow.

"Sounds wise." Tank carefully transferred cooled pralines into a cardboard box. "Here, try one." He handed one of the sugary nut-filled confections to Mike, who promptly popped it into her mouth and moaned.

Ryder could have kissed the big Cajun. His disagreement with Mike regarding her safety wasn't completely settled, but he'd gotten a reprieve. It was enough. He and Mike loaded Tank's van with Janelle's help, and they were on their way to the community center a few minutes later. Although a short ride, Ryder savored having Mike on the back of his bike, her arms wrapped around him. He parked next to the van in the over-flowing lot. The convention had grown since that first year when he'd known almost everyone in attendance. And based on Janelle's comment about his embarrassing scene, even those who hadn't been there had heard what happened. Didn't matter. If Mike was going to the convention, he'd be there, too.

Ryder grabbed a box of treats and followed Tank inside, Mike between them.

The center had been transformed. A long runway jutted out from a stage, draped with black shiny curtains that hung from the ceiling. More draping covered the walls of the space, where vendors displayed racks of fetish wear and tables of kinky tools and sexy books. People milled about, their chatter filling the cavernous space, but almost every folding chair along the runway had been claimed. Even the back rows were starting to fill in.

"Stay close," Ryder told Mike when she paused to inspect some feather and jeweled masks.

Mike frowned but moved along with her catering box to where Tank was already arranging platters and trays. She handed her box to him. Ryder set his on a corner of the table.

"You know this is a ticketed event." Mike narrowed her eyes at him. "They let me in under a press pass, but I'm not sure how you're going to be able to stay. I'm pretty sure it's sold out."

Her smirk was like a slap—pushing him away when she literally had stumbled onto a murder victim less than an hour earlier.

"He can stay with me." Tank slid the second box of pralines under the table. "The food goes quick, and I'll need help refilling."

Ryder twitched his eyebrow up. Her little play to get rid of him thwarted.

"I'm going to interview some of the vendors." Mike backed away.

A woman, loose dark hair parted down the middle and a scowl that could freeze water, barreled towards them. Ryder reached for Mike, pulling her out of the path.

"Henry? What are *you* doing here?" she snarled through glossy red lips.

With Mike in his arms, Ryder faced the harpy attacking Tank.

"Val." Tank's single syllable response hung like blade in the air.

"I told the committee *not* to use you." The woman tapped the red stiletto that peeped out from under her snug black jumpsuit.

"Guess they like my food more than they like listening to you." He smiled fully. "Can't say I disagree. Run along, Val. I got work to do." Tank turned his back, and a moment later the woman stomped away.

"That's the woman who hosted the spanking demonstration," Mike hissed.

"Take it you know her?" Ryder asked Tank.

"Ex-wife. Valerie LeBlanc, now Broussard. She's the reason for this convention being in Daisy. And its dopey farm-themed name."

"Seriously?" Mike freed herself from Ryder's grasp. "Your ex-wife put the convention in Daisy to follow you?"

"It was an amicable divorce. *Was*. She hadn't met Tony yet. After the location she'd been planning to use fell through, I invited her to come across the river. Told her I'd help her with some of the logistics and the food. Bay Leaves was just getting off the ground, so I figured it would be good exposure for me too. You remember, Ryder."

He did. Unfortunately.

"That year it didn't have the furries. That came after Val hooked up with Tony, the shithead. Although how their kinks ever mesh, I'll never know. That's why we got divorced. I'm not a Dom or a submissive, and our sex life was in the toilet. We met far too young anyway."

"Her husband is a furry?" Ryder asked.

"He's the tiger," Mike whispered and glanced up wide-eyed.

Ryder wasn't sure it was true, but if it was, they had the name of the victim: Tony Broussard.

"People, take your seats." Val's voice boomed over the microphone. "The much-anticipated fashion show is about to begin."

Heavy bass music filled the air. Olive strutted out in a cobalt blue leather bustier with a black mini skirt and high-heeled boots with heavy tread that laced up to her knees. She had on a black cap over her tightly pinned blond hair and aviator sunglasses. Val read from a card about the clothing and which vendor was selling each part of the outfit as Olive walked the runway. She paused at the end and whipped out a set of hand-cuffs to cheers from the crowd.

Ryder itched to get out of there as memories of his own *"trip down the runway"* and the ensuing *"em-bare-ass-ment"* tormented him. But Mike had out her notebook, and there would be no getting her out of there until the last model walked.

Too bad Daisy was in a dry county.

CHAPTER SIX

Mike made some final notes about the outfits that had been showcased for the last hour as the music faded. DJ Slick yanked his earphones off, and Val took center stage again.

"Thank you all for attending. Be sure to visit our lovely vendors, some of whom you saw featured in the show. I know there are a couple of items I want to get my hands on." She laughed, but it rang fake. Probably because Mike didn't find any of the outfits more appealing than her plain white t-shirt, skinny jeans, and especially her high-tops. "Don't forget—the Racy Regatta later this afternoon. Check out the parade of boats, and be sure to vote for your favorite. We'll announce the winner on Saturday at our BDSM night at the Pink Petals. It's sure to be a spanking good time and very…inspirational."

The husk in her voice made Mike's stomach turn. The woman's husband was dead, but likely she had no idea. Had they made up after their fight at the dance competition? When would the police inform her? Mike let the questions go. She had a conference to write about and her best friend's wedding to shepherd. But if she could help solve the crime and clear things up more quickly, she absolutely would.

Ryder appeared at her elbow with a plate of food. "Saved you some before the hordes decimated what was left."

"Thank you." Mike tilted her face up.

He gave her a chaste kiss. "You know I love taking care of you."

He did. But if she came to rely on him too much, what would she do when it was over? And it would end. Everybody left. Even her parents had abandoned her. Better to keep some boundaries. She scarfed down the small plate. "Want to go shopping with me?"

"Only if you let me buy you something to wear tomorrow night to the Petals party."

Mike mentally inventoried the clothes in her closet. She shouldn't, but "okay" came out of her mouth before she could stop it. "But I don't want to miss the boat parade."

"How'd you like to be on a boat during the parade?"

"You can do that?" Of course he could. He was Ryder.

One phone call later, and they had a spot on his daddy-biker friend's BDSM boat.

"I'm not calling you Daddy," she teased. And she sure as hell wasn't acting like his little girl. Nothing wrong with that, but she was too busy practicing being an adult.

Ryder smiled. "I could get you to call me anything I want, and you know it."

She did. The man was an orgasm wizard.

"But you know that's not my kink, M."

Mike balled up her paper plate and napkin and shot it into the nearby trash can.

"Still got a perfect hook." He tugged her to his side. "Let's go shopping."

He escorted her to the first booth filled with leather pants, vests, and what looked like spiked dog collars. The man there would have been at home on their assigned boat. His long beard met his chest hair between the parted sides of his leather vest.

Before Mike could talk to the guy, Ryder pulled her to the next booth that had racks of clothing that appeared to be leftover strips of leather held together by lace and netting.

"Perfect," Ryder said as he flipped through the hangers, boxes of high heels like the kind strippers wore stacked to his side.

Mike shuddered at the prospect of trying to walk in heels again. "No shoes."

"Correct. You will be barefoot." His tone—the one he only ever used when they were alone—settled right between her legs.

"Wait, what? I can't go barefoot."

"So you do want shoes?" His devilish look was a straight up challenge.

She cringed.

"No? Then quit managing and let me do this, M."

Fine. It was only one night, and at least she'd blend. Maybe he'd pick something that went with her high tops. She craned her neck to see what other options were there, besides kinky clothes and leather.

After Ryder paid the woman running the booth, they moved along the row. Lube and dildos, every battery-operated toy, including some very expensive fucking machines, were featured. Who knew a person could literally be drilled? Mike jotted down a few notes. When they got to the stand tucked in the corner, she froze.

Besides the leather skirts and vests and crops, there on the display were two leather dildos. A chill raised the hair on Mike's arms. Leather filled with sand, Chuck had explained at the spanking demo. The bloody rag and trails of sand flashed like a photo before her eyes. Is that what was used to kill Tiger Beat? Or Tony Broussard, as Tank had unknowingly informed her.

A woman who looked like she spent most of her time on a ranch, wiry and sun-dried, sat in a chair hand-sewing a pattern along the edge of a leather bra.

"Excuse me," Mike said.

"Oh, hey there. How y'all doin'?" The woman set down her sewing as she stood. "Can I help you find something? Answer any questions?"

Mike pointed at the leather tubes. "Do you sell a lot of these?"

The woman picked up the black one and thumped it in her hand. "A few. Mostly through my web store." She handed it to Mike. "They're surprisingly versatile. The leather warms with handling, and the sand gives it weight," she said, pointing to the next booth. "Chuck likes hers for spanking her sub. But it can be used to tease and even fuck. Although most people cover it with a condom in that case."

"Have you sold any at this show?" Her answer could be an important lead.

"Not this year, but it's still early. Mainly it's been clothing. People love showing off new outfits for the parade." The woman's chuckle was like dry leaves scraping down the sidewalk.

"Do you mind if I include your shop in my article? I write for *The Daily Peat.*"

"I'd be grateful for the publicity." She handed Mike a business card and then gave one to Ryder. "I do special orders."

"Sand filled?" Ryder asked, as he tucked the card in the pocket of his jeans.

"You betcha. Got a little give to it." She held out the dildo.

Ryder took it and smacked it down on his hand a couple of times. He caught Mike's eye, and she was certain he agreed that type of tool was the murder weapon.

Mike led them over to Chuck's table. There was an array of wood dildos polished to a high shine. Chuck paused her carving. "Mike. Ryder. Good to see you. Enjoying the conference?"

Ryder grunted.

"I didn't know you carved wooden…uh…" Mike wasn't sure what the appropriate word was.

"Cocks?"

"Yeah. They're beautiful." Mike trailed her finger along the smooth cherrywood artwork.

"Prettier than the real thing." Chuck laughed. "No offense, Ryder."

"None taken. And mine's prettier." Ryder nudged Mike.

Mike couldn't disagree.

Chuck laughed again. "I'll take your word for it."

"How does a fly-tying fisherman get into carving cocks?" Mike asked. Which was better than "Did you kill Tony?" the question she swallowed in the name of discretion. But really, why use sand-filled leather if there was a wooden cock-club just as readily available? And why use a dildo at all?

"At first it was curiosity. Just to see if I could do it."

Seriously? Mike flinched. But Chuck was answering the question she'd asked out loud, not the ones rattling in her head. Carving, not killing.

"My dad had always whittled, animals mostly. Being a teenager in the Texas boonies, and one without an attraction to men, well, let's just say I was motivated."

Mike nodded. It made sense on so many levels. "But these are works of art."

"Aw. I just cut away the wood that shouldn't be there so I'm left with the woody that should be."

Ryder barked a laugh.

"No way I could ever do that." Mike couldn't imagine trying to carve wood with a sharp knife. "Probably cut myself the first try."

"It happens. Usually only if I'm distracted."

Ryder whispered in her ear, "Want one?"

Hell yes, she wanted one, just to own a gorgeous wooden dick, but it seemed frivolous. "Not for me, but I think it could be the perfect bachelorette gift for Heather. You know, a one-of-a-kind sexy toy?"

Mike picked one out—a nubby rosewood that had twists carved into the middle. Ryder insisted on paying. She would have argued more, but she hadn't anticipated the price of the artwork. Chuck offered to get it gift boxed.

"Go check out the last few booths while I take care of this." Ryder nudged Mike. "Then we can get something more substantial to eat before we have to get on the boat."

After a few minutes at each booth, Ryder led her out of the community center and over to Jerry's for the best burger in Texas. That's what his menu said, and Mike couldn't think of a reason he was wrong. She followed Ryder up the ramp of the faded wood building and through the once-red entry.

"Close the door!" the patrons called out the traditional greeting. The first time Mike heard it, she'd been shocked. If there came a time when she visited and they didn't say it, she'd be devastated.

Two green-chile cheeseburgers with bacon and a side of large fries arrived quickly at the picnic table they shared with Frank McCready, the fire chief for Daisy.

Ryder pushed the fries closer to Mike and chatted with Frank. "Any drama with the convention in town?"

"You mean aside from the Bloom with a View…situation?"

"You know about that?" Ryder stiffened, back ramrod straight.

"Of course." Frank leaned closer to Ryder. "Between you and me, the guy was an ass. Should have seen him at the Tool Shed. Right in front of his wife, too."

"You were there?" Mike hadn't seen him.

"Uh yeah. I was the Dalmatian." His cheeks turned pink. "I got the outfit used—as a prank—but it's fun to participate in both worlds during the conference."

"How cool. Sorry I missed you."

"I should have said hello, but I had something else I needed to take care of." Frank popped the last bite of his burger into his mouth.

"Chuck and Berta Ann were outstanding." Mike was still amazed the deputy went so public.

Frank gathered up his trash. "Got to get back to it. Good to see you, Ryder. Mike."

With the chief out of earshot, Mike asked Ryder, "Do you think Chuck could have done it? I mean the dildo. The sand."

"She'd need a bigger motive than some inappropriate comments at a demo."

"We should find out if she had one."

Ryder crossed his arms and leveled a warning glare.

"Ryder, the gossip has already started. People know. Everyone except his wife. Chuck could be involved. Which means Berta Ann is involved. What if they're being setup to be falsely accused?"

Ryder grunted.

"And we don't know this sheriff at all."

"That doesn't mean we should get involved."

It wasn't a no. She just needed a stronger argument. "That's exactly why we should. This is your town. The people here love you. They count on you. And Heather is counting on me. I can't let her wedding take place in the middle of an unsolved crime scene. Even if she forgave me, I would never forgive myself for not doing everything I could."

Ryder took another bite of his burger, chewing thoughtfully. He sipped his water. "Fine. But you have to stick close. I won't have you at risk."

"Of course." She muffled the frisson of excitement that shot through her like electricity. "After we finish, I need to go by the *Peat*. Transcribe some of my notes."

"Perfect. I'll go with you and help you get changed for the parade." Ryder's voice was full of sexy innuendo. "We can talk about the rest of the convention schedule."

"You don't really have to go to *all* the events with me." Although she did like having Ryder by her side. He knew everyone, and she wouldn't have to be on guard like all single women in a crowd. But she shouldn't need him that way. And she didn't want him blocking her investigation.

"M. We talked about this. You're going to dig into the murder. You can't help yourself. I have to know you're safe." He grazed his fingers over hers. "Don't push me away."

His comment stung. She wasn't trying to push him away, just control her dependence on him. "I have a printed copy of the schedule at the office."

Ryder cleared their empty baskets and followed her back to the *Peat*.

RYDER TOOK a seat in the only comfortable seat in the office of *The Daily Peat*. He didn't have to worry about breaking the overstuffed, blue living room–style chair.

"Let me grab the flyer, and you can look at it while I type up my notes." Mike jogged down the long hallway of the shotgun-style house.

He picked up one of the photos from the built-in shelves Mike had filled with her mementos. The image was a gangly, teenage version of his girlfriend hugging her brother, the man whose suicide Ryder was still digging into. There were new leads according to his brief discussion with Ike. Once they were on the boat, Ryder would get more details. He carefully replaced the photo next to the other images, one of her brother surrounded by his military buddies—posed exactly like his own pictures. But Ryder didn't put his on display for lots of reasons.

Down the long hall in her bedroom, Mike shuffled through a pile of papers. The newspaper occupied the front room, but that hadn't stopped them from having sex there—multiple times.

Most memorably the night she got the job, right up against the wall next to the front door. Ryder shifted. He'd love to strip Mike down and make love to her this afternoon, but he couldn't skip out on his buddy after calling in a favor. Besides, Mike's bed was far too narrow and short for...anything.

"Here." Mike handed him a folded glossy brochure done in blue and black with a cow head logo wearing a cowbell around its neck and a riding crop hovering diagonally above. Ryder snorted. He'd seen worse logos, but not many.

She nudged the photo he'd moved a tiny bit. "I'll be quick."

"Take as long as you need."

She darted back down the hall and opened her laptop at the built-in desk.

He flipped open the brochure to the list of events for the weekend. Luckily, the boat parade was the halfway mark. He'd only have to deal with the second half of the convention, mostly classes, an event at the Pink Petals, and finally on Sunday, a service at the New Life interdenominational church. Ryder chuckled. It was the South. Nothing started or ended without at least one blessing, and he didn't figure the Baptists, the only other church in town, were going to welcome the kinky leather-and-fur-wearing crowd to their place on Sunday.

He set the paper aside and stretched out his legs. None of the remaining events gave Ryder cause for concern, so it was just a matter of getting Mike to tell him what she planned to attend. With his hands folded over his chest, he closed his eyes to catch a quick nap.

"HEY, YOU." Mike rubbed Ryder's shoulder, and he caught her hand and tugged her into his lap. She squeaked and swatted his chest. "I thought you were asleep."

"I was until you came into the room." His grin sent heat pulsing through her.

"I don't get how you do that. Are you ready to go to the marina?"

"I need to swing by the shop."

"We should get your bike anyway." Mike didn't like the idea of leaving it overnight at the center. Too much had happened there that summer.

"Yeah, I'd rather take the truck tonight."

"Or we could take my car?" That way she could be in control for a change.

Ryder rolled his eyes. "Only if I can take out the passenger seat and sit in the back."

Once again, he pointed out how he didn't fit in her life and she'd have to adapt to his. "It's not that small."

"Did you decide on tomorrow's sessions?"

Mike let him change the subject and rattled off a few, including one about abuse.

"Abuse?"

"Recognizing the signs of an unhealthy power exchange in a relationship. When Kink Starts to Stink."

"Good call. What about Sunday services?"

"I haven't decided. Maybe. Is that okay?" They didn't go to church, and Mike wasn't even sure if Ryder was a believer. She'd been more diligent before her brother's death, but never a regular.

"Of course. I go to church."

"When?"

"Sunday, apparently." He tugged her hair. "You should let me braid this for you. And I got you a new t-shirt to wear."

"Really?" She jumped off his lap and raced to where he'd left the bags on the desk.

Ryder beat her to them. "Wait. Let me show you."

"So bossy." Which she kind of loved, despite her best efforts.

He fished around in the clothing bag and pulled out the black cotton. Then held it up for her to read. In big letters it had "I Need a Hug" and then in smaller type "e dick inside me."

Mike burst out laughing and grabbed it. "It's perfect." She whipped off the plain shirt she'd been wearing, not at all sad when Ryder's eyes locked on her lace-clad breasts. She took the opportunity to play with him, adjusting each breast in her bra then sliding her arms into the sleeves. Once she had the tee over her head, she slowly shifted the fabric down, smoothing each wrinkle. "Okay. Ready."

Ryder shot her a heated look full of promise and landed a sharp slap on her ass. Her body lit up, but no time for fun and games.

They walked over to the center and took Ryder's bike back to his place. He changed into a leather vest and black jeans. Damn. Leather was an entirely different level of sexy. He styled Mike's hair in a quick French braid. She slid in close on the bench seat of his old truck as he drove them into town, past the Bloom with a View, to the lake's marina.

His buddy's boat was right where he'd said—a sleek, white sailboat flying a skull and crossbones flag. Red and black banner flags decorated the silver railing that surrounded the deck. Ryder and Mike strode down the weathered dock hand in hand. In short order, Ryder was introducing Mike to a man dressed similarly to Ryder but with a blousy white shirt open to his navel underneath his vest.

"Ike, this is my girlfriend, Mike. Mike, this is the man who has saved my life more times than I deserved, Ike Packer."

"Nice to meet you, Mike." He thrust out his hand, his bare arm ripped with muscles.

Ike had to be fifteen years older than Ryder but was still in amazing shape from what Mike could see of his ebony dark skin peeking out from his shirt. Mike's hand trembled the tiniest bit before shaking his, and her breath caught in her lungs when he locked his striking green-eyed gaze on her. Who was this guy? What did Ryder mean about saving his life? An exaggeration? Were they in the military together? Or had they met somewhere else?

"You can call me Daddy Ike," he said in a deep gravelly voice.

Mike laughed. "What?"

"Knock it off," Ryder growled at his friend and plastered his warm arm around Mike's shoulders, clutching her close. "Ignore him, M. Where's the beer?"

Ike grinned. "Just testing. Come on. I'll give you a tour."

Despite the way he had used her to tease Ryder, she couldn't help but like the daddy Dom. They toured the boat's two bedrooms, bathroom, and full kitchen. Ike introduced her to the other passengers. Two women and another man, all in pirate-like costumes.

"We're gonna lash Lacy here to the mast during the parade," Ike said. "Think that could put us over on votes."

Lacy was wearing a flayed leather skirt that barely hid her G-string and an embroidered leather bra that had to be from the shop Mike and Ryder visited earlier that day.

Ike guided them back to the kitchen. "Let's get a beer. We can talk downstairs about—"

Ryder stepped in between the man and Mike. "What do you want to drink, M?"

"Tea for now."

Ryder and Ike tag-teamed on pouring her a glass from a pitcher in the fridge. "Go up on deck. I know you want to take some notes on the other boats." Ryder nudged her toward the open stairs. "I'll be up shortly, and we can watch the sunset together."

"So romantic," Ike teased.

Mike went up the stairs, but she lingered just outside the opening, out of Ryder's view. Something was up. She should have paid more attention when Ryder had called to get them on the boat. Seemed like Ryder and Ike had already planned to meet.

"What'd you hear?" Ryder's voice was barely audible.

Mike crouched down.

"I figured out why they called in the INL. Besides the boats coming in, the coke was being shipped across multiple states. Could still be for all we know."

"From Daisy?"

"I-10 ain't far away, brother. And you got a body problem in this town."

Ryder mumbled something.

"I know. But rumor is they had protection. That's how they were getting away with growing and importing and everything else. Might need to get ex to look into it. I'll reach out. Let you know."

Ex? Maybe she'd misheard.

"…suicide?"

Dang it. Mike wished she was down below, but there was no way they would talk in front of her. But between Ryder's last comment and the mention of International Narcotics and Law where David had worked, they had to be talking about her brother.

Her chest ached, battling the anger over being excluded and the relief that Ryder was still digging into what happened to David. And what if the murders in Daisy—because somehow Ike knew about the tiger—were related? She planned to find out.

The slapping of hands and mumbling of thanks had Mike scrambling to get away from the door before they caught her eavesdropping. Ryder and Ike emerged just as music blared from some speakers. It sounded like Viking death metal. Not quite pirate-y, but it kind of worked for BDSM pirates.

"It's time," squealed Lacy as she raced barefoot to the mast. "Quick, Daddy. Tie me up."

Ike laughed and held out a black cotton rope as he stomped toward her. Ryder pressed against Mike's back and wrapped his arms around her middle. "Having fun?"

"So far." Did Ryder know she'd been eavesdropping?

"Let's go check out the other boats."

She wasn't going to confess. Instead, she held up her phone. "Selfie?"

Ryder smiled and bent down to fit in the photo.

Themed boats were assembling in a mostly orderly fashion to take their turn in the spotlight. The furries had the leg up on decorating. There was a Noah's ark, a zoo, even some childhood book themes based on the two-headed llama. But the most impressive was the circus that had aerial performers in leather gear. It was a brilliant combination of the two main kinks represented at the conference. Although the main ring on the ship seemed to be missing one of its animals. No lion or tiger. Instead, there was a teddy bear trying to act fierce for a Domme dressed all in red with gold accents. Mike snapped pictures with her phone. When it came time for their pirate boat's turn, everyone had a role and took their place, except for her and Ryder.

"What should we do?"

"Get on your knees."

Sassy comebacks wrestled with her clenched teeth. No time, and she didn't want to ruin Ike's chance of winning. Ryder tugged her hair and held her close to his groin with his legs spread wide apart. She was sure she looked totally submissive and had to keep from laughing at the image that formed in her brain.

"You'll ruin it," Ryder said. Mirth danced just below the stern expression he tried to hold. Moments later, they were on the move again, and Mike flopped on the deck laughing. Ryder could pull off being a sexy Dom, but Mike could never be a believable sub in a BDSM vignette.

As the sun settled behind the horizon of trees, reflecting on the water and painting the soft-blue sky in vivid shades of orange and yellow, the parties only got wilder. Louder music, squeals and screams, and dancing that may have crossed the carnal line.

"Should we get Ike to take us back?" Mike asked Ryder. Their host was currently dirty dancing with Lacy while spanking her bare ass for all to see. Then he untied Lacy's bra and it dropped to the ground.

"He seems a little busy right now." Ryder raised an eyebrow. "But we can go downstairs. I know this isn't your scene."

"Guess I should have expected—"

Ryder spun her toward the opening that led into the hull. "I've been waiting all evening to put that bedroom to use. Ever had sex on a boat?"

CHAPTER SEVEN

Mike wasn't sure what time it was, but the weak light coming through the tiny porthole windows said early. The lapping water against the gently rocking hull of the boat could lull her back to sleep, but Ryder lay next to her—glorious, naked, and tempting. She traced the line of his back with a single finger from his neck, slowly reaching for the sheet that covered his ass. Before she could move it aside and get a view of his very taut backside, he moved like a lightning flash, and she was under him with her hands held above her head.

She arched her back to relieve the delicious tension of his possession.

"Mmm," he grunted before pressing his lips to hers and then to her neck and along her chest, leaving a trail of tingles. He paused to tease one of her still-sensitive nipples, his shadow of a beard rough on her skin. He wedged a leg between hers, his thigh pressing against her aching pussy.

Oh damn. This was just like the previous night—when he'd done wicked things to her body—continued.

After tasting her other breast and giving it a light nip, he moved his hands to cup them. His heat sizzled through her skin and into her blood. With soft, slow kisses, he shimmied down her belly. His lips tickled and tormented her with anticipation. She wriggled, her body still on a knife's edge from all the orgasms he'd given her only hours ago.

"Hold still," he demanded.

"I can't." She shifted her hips, seeking him. Desperate for more, despite being totally sated.

"Should I stop?"

She glared at him. "I think you might be a sadist."

His wicked grin was beyond translation but promised so many pleasures. She parted her legs farther and went boneless, letting him own her because he was so very good at taking care of her. And damn, was that what it would be like to live with him? Nonstop, panty-drenching bliss?

He lifted her legs and kissed each inner thigh thoroughly from her knee to her begging sex. But not where she craved his touch. He was testing her, based on the glint in his wicked brown eyes and the arch of his brow, but she remained still and let him do what he would. Finally, his tongue found the path to her clit, and in minutes, she would have agreed to anything he wanted. Sucking and licking, he used his lips and tongue and finally even his fingers to push her beyond coherence. He tugged her sensitive nub between his lips and pressed his thumb against her ass. His taboo touch shot her into the random space where ecstasy lived and Mike floated.

"Stars."

Ryder laughed then kissed her slowly, blanketing her with his body.

"We should stay here all day," Mike said with a sigh.

"You'll miss your conference."

"You're right." And he was, but she didn't move.

"I'll buy you breakfast at Bay Leaves."

Her stomach growled. "Done. But I have to change first. I can't wear that shirt in front of Janelle."

"Yeah, a shower would be good, too. Let me check with Ike and see when he's planning to dock."

Ryder stood, and the boat started moving. He slapped a hand to the wall and stayed upright. "Guess we're going now."

———

SEATED AT THE BAY LEAVES, Mike's mouth watered as she dug into her grits and grillades—the slow-cooked pork melting in her mouth—when a woman with dark hair askew, make-up smudged, and wrinkled clothes ran in screaming.

"Where are you? You son of a bitch. I know you did this." She spun in the center of the restaurant, eyes wild. "Henry Murphy, you get your ass out here. I'm gonna kill you."

Tank appeared from the kitchen, and Ryder stood. Berta Ann was in uniform, dining with Chuck. They pushed back from their table and rose. The screeching woman was the Domme from the spanking demo, the dead tiger's wife, Val Broussard.

She stabbed her finger into Tank's chest. "You hated him. Just because he understood me. You hated him, and you killed him. I know it."

"Val, hold on." Tank held his hands up.

Berta Ann reached for the woman's arm. "Ma'am."

Val spun and slapped Berta Ann so hard Mike felt the impact. Chuck took a step, hands balled into fists, but Berta Ann shook her head.

"Now you're under arrest for assault and battery *and* assaulting an officer." Berta Ann slapped a cuff on one wrist and wrenched the woman's other arm back to click the second cuff in place.

Val, suddenly silent, struggled in the cuffs. Berta Ann spun her toward the door without a hint of effort.

"Tank, gonna need you to come by the station sometime

today and make a statement. In the meantime, she's coming with me." Berta Ann recited the woman's rights as she escorted her detainee from the restaurant.

Headline: Decked Deputy Detains Dumb Domme

"Chuck?" Ryder's voice was completely calm, despite the excitement. "You need a ride?"

"Not necessary. I could use the walk. But thanks." She returned to the table and continued to eat, getting a box from the server for Berta Ann's breakfast.

Ryder returned to Mike.

"What the heck was all that about?" she asked. Tank couldn't have killed Tony. Well, technically, he could have. He had the size to pull it off. And he'd been at the spanking demo—he could have taken the leather dildo, assuming it was missing. He'd also tried to keep her from measuring the field for the tent. If he really was upset over Val—

No. Tank was a gentle giant. Mike just couldn't see him doing it. "There's no way Tank would have killed his ex-wife's husband."

"Sometimes people surprise you."

"Lots of people were at the spanking demo. Not just Tank. And we don't know that it was Chuck's tool that was used." Mike glanced over, but Chuck was already leaving.

"Most of the people at the conference know Tony and his wife. Not to mention, it could have all been a show to prove her innocence." Ryder sipped his coffee.

"Wow. I didn't think of that. But she showed how strong she was. That slap was brutal."

A shadow settled over their table. Tank. "Sorry you had to see that."

"Are you okay?" Mike asked.

"My ex-wife." He shrugged as if that explained everything.

Could just meeting another guy, after she and Tank were already divorced, be enough to make Val so hateful? Mike had questions. "But something must have happened between you and Tony. Why else would she think you killed him?"

"I'm sure I don't know what," Tank said. "Just wanted to thank you, Ryder, for being at the ready. Breakfast is on me."

"You don't have to—"

Tank held up his hand, cutting Ryder off. He lumbered back to his kitchen, shoulders hunched, head dropped. Berta Ann had been the one to take the slap, but Tank was the beaten man.

Mike was more convinced than ever that she had to find out who really did this. A rumor that Tank was a killer could destroy the Bay Leaves and her favorite Cajun chef, not to mention ruin Heather's wedding. The best way to find out who else could have done it was to get back to the convention—the event that had brought the victim and the killer together. She licked the last of the grits off her fork. "Ready? We need to get to the fire station."

"What's happening there?"

As if he'd forgotten. "Chief McCready is going to give a demo and tips on safe fire play."

FUCK. Ryder closed his eyes briefly. Fire play. Even he didn't experiment with that kind of danger. He'd seen the effects of fire, and it wasn't at all sexual to him. But people probably felt that way about his kinks. And it wasn't like he'd let Mike go alone. She was bound and determined to investigate the murder, putting herself at risk. He pushed away from the table, dropped some twenties on top, and followed Mike out the door. It was going to be a long day.

When they pulled up to the fire station, the town fire engine was parked on the street and folding chairs filled one half of the driveway facing into the garage.

"There's a couple of seats up front." Mike bounced out of

Ryder's old truck and raced to claim the prime seating. Ryder noted Olive and Weenie were both in the audience and, despite being half sisters, as far apart as two people could be. He nodded to Ike and Lacy as he passed. The people sitting farther back had the right idea as far as Ryder was concerned, but Mike waved him over and he dutifully took his place.

Frank McCready faced the audience, and slowly the conversations died down. "Thank you for coming to this Cowbells and Crops seminar. I'm sorry to be doing my own introduction, but my hostess slash demonstration partner hasn't arrived, and I only have a short time to spend with you." He glanced around as if hoping Val, who was listed on the event details, would appear. After the scene at the Bay Leaves, Ryder was confident she'd be missing the event.

"I'm Chief McCready, and this morning we'll be discussing fire play, specifically the safety issues and type of fire play most commonly practiced in the community. I'll do a small demonstration at the end and, later tonight, there will be a longer scene at the Pink Petals. But this is the time to ask your questions."

Mike leaned over to Ryder. "I can't wait to write this up. Nobody talks about fire play. Hey, isn't that Officer Kessler?"

Ryder turned to the right and glanced back. Kessler, arms crossed over his khaki uniform, gave him a nod. Strange. He would have thought the man would have his hands full with Tank's ex-wife. Then again, Berta Ann was a badass who could have been the sheriff if she'd wanted to. The only reason his cousin had the job was Berta Ann refused to take it.

"Who here has practiced any kind of fire play?" the chief's voice boomed out over the audience.

Olive and another couple raised their hands.

The chief nodded. "I'll bet more of you've been tempted. Ever lit the room with just candles to create a sexy atmosphere? Tried wax play? How about a massage with cupping?" The chief held up two glass containers that looked like small, rounded jelly jars. "It's popular with the alternative health crowd, but cupping can be a type of fire play if it's used in that context."

Mike scribbled in her notebook, and Ryder tried to sit still. Lectures in general made him nuts—he'd much rather be doing instead of listening to someone *talk* about doing. In the case of fire, he'd much rather be as far away as possible.

"First thing with any dangerous play—and fire *is* dangerous —you must prepare for safety." The chief held up a folded white piece of fabric. "This is a fire blanket." He snapped it open. "This is for putting out fire on people." He put the blanket down and picked up a red canister. "You must have a fire extinguisher. Preferably a class B disposable, less than five years old. Check that the pressurization gauge is in the green. Don't assume. Use this for anything on fire that isn't human." After setting the canister on the ground, he glanced around the crowd. "I'll need a volunteer."

To Ryder's horror, Mike raised her hand, and the chief invited her up before he could put a stop to it. The woman had *zero* sense of self-preservation.

"Mike's a good volunteer today for a couple of reasons."

None that Ryder could think of.

"She's wearing cotton. Her shirt and jeans will get a hole if the fire touches them, but they won't melt into her skin. Also, the shirt is form fitting."

The man needed to take his eyes off Mike's tits. Immediately.

"Normally, if I'm practicing for personal pleasure, my play-mate will not be troubled with items of clothing."

Ryder growled and rolled his hands into fists.

"Caleb is standing by to assist in the unlikely event we should have any unexpected situations."

The audience chuckled, and Mike blushed. Ryder gritted his teeth. Not that he didn't trust the Petal's bouncer to take action if needed, but there better not be any *unexpected situations*. The chief continued on, showing his fire wands and talking about the type of fire play he could do with them and even the various types of fuel. He explained what he would do during the demo, stroking his hand up Mike's arm. "Mike, are you still okay to act as my volunteer?"

Mike nodded.

Ryder shifted in his chair and scowled.

"I need your verbal consent."

"Yes, I want to volunteer for the fire play demonstration."

Then Chief McCready soaked one of the fire wands in isopropyl alcohol and lit it on fire. He held Mike's arm out and tapped the flame down her arm, wiping any areas that stayed lit for more than a second.

"Oh." Mike stared at her arm. "It stings a bit."

Not as much as her ass was going to when Ryder lit it up with his hand. Not only was she once again involved in a murder investigation, but she'd volunteered to be set on fire. He checked out the audience again, assessing their reaction to his girlfriend's crazy behavior. Olive smirked at him. Ryder shook his head and rolled his eyes before returning his attention to Mike.

"Let's give Mike a round of applause for being my willing sub."

A round of enthusiastic clapping raked up Ryder's spine. He and McCready would have a conversation about that *my sub* comment. Later. In private.

Mike bounced into her chair as the chief answered questions. "Oh, my god. That was so fun." She held out her arm. "Look, it didn't even leave a mark. Except now I might need to wax my other arm to match."

Ryder made a noncommittal sound and crossed his arms. He'd be keeping an eye on the chief after hitting on his girl like that. So what if she'd volunteered. He didn't have to be logical when it came to his feelings for Mike.

Mike pulled out her notebook. "Next session. There's Kinky Yoga at the Tool Shed, or Oral Sex Tips at the library, or Bring Your Furry to Life. I think we decided on yoga, but I'm not sure we're dressed for it, and I'm still full from breakfast."

"Lady's choice."

"Oral sex."

"That's what you always choose." Ryder gave her a sexy grin.

Mike slapped at his arm playfully. "Never heard you complain."

"No man alive complains when he gets oral."

"I'm sure somewhere someone has. Like if it was terrible."

"Doubt it." He'd be willing to suffer a bad blowjob if it would get him out of another class.

Mike rose. "Come on. Let's get to the library. I don't want to be late to class."

"Yeah, probably get late fees." Ryder followed her through the crowd. Whispers about Val and Tony hit his ears. Apparently, the cat was out of the bag. Or in the body bag, as it were.

The hour-long oral sex class was divided in two. The first half covered fellatio, and the second cunnilingus. And Ryder had learned more about the Latin definitions and techniques than one person should be subjected to. The only result was that he had no desire for oral sex for about the next year. The two presenters had been so clinical it was like getting the pre-op discussion from the doc on what's happening with the colonoscopy. And yeah, they'd blown plenty of air up peoples' asses because they'd forgotten to mention how fun oral sex was. They said the word pleasure. But he had his doubts as to their experience.

Mike nudged him as soon as they stepped outside. "That was—"

"Boring."

"Yeah. How did they make it boring?" Mike's face wrinkled like she'd smelled a turd.

A laugh burst into their private bubble. Chuck. "I was thinking the same thing. Next year, I'm teaching the pussy eating. That fucker didn't know what he was talking about."

Ryder laughed.

"Hey, did you hear how Tony died?" Mike asked.

Ryder blinked. Mike had *not* just asked that.

"No." Chuck leaned closer. "I'd heard someone died. Kind of put it together after breakfast."

"Are you—did your spanking thing—tool, whatever—" Mike flicked her hand in the air.

"My leather dildo?"

"Yeah. Is it missing?" Mike asked.

"I don't think so. Why?"

Ryder had to intervene. "Mike."

Chuck snapped her gaze to Ryder. "I'll check and let you know."

Ryder nodded.

"Oh. Okay," Mike said as Chuck marched off.

Ryder frowned. That had not been the best way to find out about the possible murder weapon. "We don't know who's been interviewed and what's common knowledge."

"Right. Sorry." She shrugged. "But it's Chuck."

He gave her the look.

Mike's cheeks pinkened, and she flipped open her notebook. "So, we have a lunch break, and after, we can choose from Basic Sewing—repair and fur suit design—at the community center, or a *Shibari* demo. There's also a food one at the Flour Bed, but—"

"Phō King?"

"Nope. That's not on the list." She released a tentative chuckle.

"Come on, M. Let's get you fed." Still on foot, he held her hand as they made their way back to the main road and the strip mall where Giang and his sister Tan had their restaurant, one of

Mike's favorites. The name always made her smile, and Ryder would do anything to keep her smiling.

After Mike finished eating her weight in noodles and vegetables, like she hadn't had a huge breakfast, she leaned back in her chair. "I don't think I could look at another bite of food right now."

"So much for the Flour Bed sexy food demo. That leaves fur suit fixing or fancy rope tying." Ryder preferred the *Shibari* demo, but he stifled it because this was her show.

"You don't need rope tricks." Mike grinned.

"I don't need to fix a furry costume either."

"I feel like I've covered a bunch of the BDSM side of the conference."

"Sewing class it is." Ryder had avoided home economics in school, but he could sew a button back on in a pinch, yet somehow, he'd volunteered himself for costume repair. Mike was dangerous to his sanity. And he loved it.

When they entered the center, the demonstration seemed to have been forgotten. People, garbed in a mix of street clothes, club wear, and full or partial fur suits, milled around in groups of twos and threes.

Letty rushed over to them, slide-on heels clopping. Wasn't she supposed to be teaching a food thing? Before Ryder could react, Mike walked away. Ryder whipped his gaze back and forth between Mike and the baker. Letty's flirting was harmless, but Mike couldn't be convinced.

Letty clung to Ryder as if they were sailing in stormy weather. "I heard what happened," she said in a long drawl. "Isn't it awful?"

Ryder averted his eyes from her exposed cleavage. "What?"

"Someone killed Tony. Val's been arrested. But I heard he got his face bashed in. How would she have done that? I mean, we women just don't have the same strength as men." She batted her false eyelashes at him.

A laugh boiled up, but Ryder held it back. He'd seen women in the military accomplish all kinds of amazing feats of strength that made beating up a man in a tiger suit seem like light work. "Who'd you hear about Tony and Val from?"

"It was all anyone could talk about right before I canceled my sensual foods demo. It just seemed disrespectful to discuss all the uses for whipped cream." The tip of her tongue teased her painted lip.

"Hmm." Ryder grunted. The woman was harmless but incorrigible. "Who exactly was leading the gossip?" He scanned the room. A lion and a bear were standing far too close to Mike.

"I really couldn't say. It was a crowd, of course. I know the fire chief was there, and so was Weenie. And Damon and Caleb never miss my demos. I think they just like free food."

The DJ and the bouncer were both were strong enough to have done the deed. They should have been working at the Pink Petals after the dance contest concluded. He'd have to find out if they knew the victim and if they were at the spanking demo. Assuming Chuck's beater was the actual murder weapon.

Ryder turned to find Mike. She had disappeared behind the lion, his paw on her shoulder, and the bear had closed in. Oh, *yiff* no. Ryder freed his arm from the baker's grasp. "Excuse me, Letty."

"Donuts tomorrow?" she called out to him.

He waved, not looking back. He had his sights on a damsel who required distressing.

MIKE CAUGHT Ryder's moving figure out of the corner of her eye. "Will you excuse me?"

But the lion and bear didn't move. She extricated herself and met Ryder a few feet from the guys.

"What are you doing, M?"

She shouldn't like that growly voice so much. "Chatting with some of the conference attendees. They were telling me about a new barbecue place. Why? What are you doing?"

"Getting information from Letty. Who's no threat."

"It's not like someone is going to attack me in the middle of this event," she scoffed. "There are thirty vendors with nothing better to do than watch what's going on."

"And yet, we have a body."

Mike shivered at the involuntary recollection that flashed before her eyes. "I know. And those two know the elephant that Tony argued with. Said he works in construction."

"Did you get a name?"

Mike sighed. "I was working on that when a wanna-be wolf started stalking me."

"Wolf? Where?" Ryder's gaze left her as he searched the room.

"Seriously?" She poked his shoulder. "*You*. I think we should take this fur suit design thing and make you a wolf costume so people can see you coming."

"I think people see *you* coming, Little Red. And they are all too happy to take advantage."

"You're ridiculous." Part of her loved his overprotectiveness. The sane part of her hated how dependent she'd become. She needed some space. Girl time. But Heather was in Houston, and if she called her, it would just be one wedding detail after another. Like the cake topper that she hadn't delivered.

She was running out of time to get everything done. "We're going to the Pink Petals tonight."

"I know."

"I need to call Shelly. See if she can do my hair and nails. Besides, Shelly might know something. Everyone spills the truth in the salon chair. And there is no safer place than the hairdresser, so no, you can't come."

"Get an appointment. I'll drive you over. But I'm not staying to sew a wolf suit. Doesn't look like the class is going to be that successful, anyway."

Mike glanced over to where the sewing machines had been set up. Three people listened to a man describe the details of getting a strong seam. Six machines and multiple chairs sat empty. "Then can you do me a favor?"

"Of course."

"I forgot to deliver the cake topper to Heather's baker. Would you be willing—"

"Yep. Where is it?"

He was too good. No wonder she relied on him so easily. Mike explained that it was on her bookcase in the main room.

"No problem. Meet you at the Root Zone?"

"I'll call you when I'm done. Might be a while." At least a couple of hours if she had her way.

Ryder grunted.

Guilt gnawed at the back of her neck. Not only was she ditching her boyfriend, but she was offloading her commitments on him. And he was going to wait for her? "What do you think everyone's doing since the food class was canceled?"

"Gossiping about who killed Tony."

She hated to miss the chatter. "What about you?"

"After I take care of Heather's cake, I'm going to talk to Officer Lance and find out what *he's* doing about catching the killer."

CHAPTER EIGHT

MIKE CLIMBED THE FEW STAIRS OUTSIDE THE ROOT ZONE. THE cute bungalow with its purple and pink door, black and white steps, and bright-yellow shutters always made Mike smile. Big turquoise pots on each side of the stairs held white chrysanthemums. She stepped inside, and the familiar smell of hairspray and nail polish remover greeted her.

"Be right with you," Shelly's voice sang out from the back over the rockabilly lyrics of Elvis's "Burning Love."

Mike crossed the warm-toned entry rag-rug and set her things down next to the manicure table. Shelly appeared from behind the curtained back room, wiping her hands on a towel that she tossed in the laundry basket next to the two wash sinks. "Hey, Mike. How are you?"

"Stressed over Heather's wedding."

Shelly plunked Mike's fingertips into soaking bowls. "How's the bride holding up? Am I still doing her hair next week?"

"I think so. I mean, if the crime scene tape is removed from her reception area."

"I heard about that. Weenie was in earlier, said one of the furries got himself killed."

"Did she tell you I found the body?" Shit. Was she supposed to tell Shelly that? Oh well.

"No." Shelly peered at Mike over her pink-framed glasses as she removed the old polish from Mike's fingertips. "Was it awful?"

Mike shivered. "It kind of was. But also like a movie. You can't really believe what you're seeing. And Donny's gone. And Berta Ann and Chuck might be involved—or someone else who was at the Tool Shed Thursday night."

"Berta Ann?" Shelly gasped.

Dang it. Mike was giving more information than she was getting. "I don't know…it's all so confusing."

Shelly switched her focus to Mike's other hand. "Did you meet Officer Kessler? I hear he's quite a hottie. Need to get him in one of my chairs."

"I met him. He *is* pretty cute. But I don't know what he's doing about the murder. He was at the fire play demo earlier."

"Don't tell me. Chief?"

"Yeah."

"That man likes his fire. Always has. Used to be the first to start the barbecue or the campfire, even when we were little kids." Shelly rolled her eyes. "He might put those fires out, but it doesn't surprise me at all that he likes to play with it."

"I let him demonstrate on me."

"Well, hell. I'd let him demonstrate on me, too. Pretty sure Letty had a go, but she's kind of against things getting burned on principle."

The chief lost attractiveness at the image of him trailing fire over Letty's body. "I guess not burning things is rule one for a baker."

"Ha. Well, it should be." Shelly had Mike's cuticles all cleaned up and was massaging lotion into her hands. That was the best part of a manicure. "What color are we doing today?"

"I'm going with Ryder to a demonstration at the Pink Petals tonight. Something bold or kinky, I guess?"

"I've got just the thing. New polish—looks red from one direction and gold from another. Kind of like flames."

"Perfect. And can you do my hair too?"

"Absolutely." Shelly retrieved the bottle from the tiny shelves mounted to the wall with polish lined up like soldiers. "I heard there was a ruckus at the Bay Leaves this morning."

"I was there. Tank's ex-wife accused him of killing her husband—the furry in the woods that I found."

"As if. Tank Murphy is a saint. Otherwise, Janelle would have nothing to do with him."

"Are they dating?"

"It's a mystery," Shelly said with a knowing smile. "But that ex-wife of his is wild. I never did understand why she married Tony. Never really had a nice word to say about him except that he would indulge her domination on occasion and he didn't care who else she slept with."

"Tony and Val had an open marriage?"

"The openest. They met at a convention."

"I heard they started it."

"Kind of. It was originally a one-time thing, sponsored by the owner of the Tool Shed along with CK. They put out some emails and got some folks together, but it was pretty much a mess."

CK, the former owner of the Pink Petals, was long gone, so no questioning him. But maybe the elusive shop owner? "The Tool Shed. Violet Savage. I'm surprised I haven't met her."

"Neither have I. Only seen her name. I think she lives out of town." Shelly released Mike's hand. "How's that?"

Mike stretched out her fingers and rotated her wrist to catch the light. The polish really did look like flames. "I love it." She placed her other hand in Shelly's, who continued polishing.

"So anyway, Val—she was a quiet thing at first. Kinda hid in

Tank's shadow, even though they were divorced. Don't get me wrong—she did the Domme thing, but outside of that, she was sweet as pie. Personally, I think she was more of a switch. You know, could go Domme or sub depending on who she's with. And Tony, that man played her. I don't know what all he had going on, but he had more secrets than a Baptist preacher."

Mike snorted.

"Each year they came out for Cowbells, she just got harsher and harsher. And he dragged younger and younger women in front of her. I don't know why she didn't leave him. But I guess now she doesn't have to." She swiped her hair back and stood. "Let's get you over to the chair. Unless…are we cutting?"

"No, just a fancy do."

"How about some braids? I did some of the hair for the fashion show, and the girls all had pictures. Found this really sexy one that would be perfect with your hair." Shelly dug through some magazines and pulled out one that had been folded open to a woman who had three braids on the side pulled into a French twist at the back. It was intricate and reminded her of the *Shibari* pictures that had been in the Cowbells brochure.

"It's perfect," Mike said, and she dropped into the chair and held her arms out as Shelly placed the cape over her, being careful not to smudge her nails. "What about Val? Was she seeing other people, too?"

"Here and there. I think most recently, she'd been hooking up with the fire chief. At least that's what Letty told me. You know, Letty once had a one-night stand with Tony, a few conferences back. She said if he was a donut, it wouldn't be a long john."

Mike laughed with Shelly. Who hadn't Letty fucked? Ryder. Which was why the woman chased him so hard. But Shelly was Letty's best friend, so Mike bit her tongue.

"Of course, he was always trying to come back for seconds,

HELL HATH NO FURRY

and she loved to flirt with him just to have the pleasure of turning him down. It was like payback for the pleasure he'd promised and failed to deliver."

"What about any of the other convention people? Any other fights or love triangles?"

"Not that I really would know."

Too direct. Mike had broken the gossip spell. She had to give some more. "I got to ride on one of the boats in the Regatta. It was so much fun."

"Really? I've always wanted to do that."

Mike regaled Shelly with tales about the BDSM boat and the others in the contest, including the circus boat, until the woman relaxed again. "Did you go to the dance competition? I was so impressed."

"Letty dragged me there."

"Did you see Tony perform? It was pretty hot."

"The man could dance. But I was shocked he didn't dance with his crew. They always do a group performance. When he won best solo and they lost group for the first time since the competition started... Well, let's just say, I think Tony was going to have to find a new crew." Shelly spun the chair to face the mirror. "What do you think?"

Mike turned her head from side to side. "Wow."

Shelly gave her a hand mirror and spun her again so she could see the back.

"This is amazing, Shelly. Thank you!" Mike paid her and gave her a hug, promising to be back to tell her all about Pink Petals.

AFTER RYDER FINISHED DELIVERING the topper, he parked in front of the sheriff's station, missing Donny not for the first time since he'd dropped him off at the airport. Instead of his helpful cousin, he had to chat with Officer Lance. Maybe he'd found something out, and really, Ryder should give him the benefit of the doubt.

"Berta Ann." Ryder lifted his hand in a friendly gesture to the deputy behind the plexiglass barrier. "Officer Kessler here?"

"Hey, Ryder. He's in the back. I'll buzz you in."

A grinding ringtone sounded, and the door to the back clicked in release. Ryder headed down the hall toward the conference room that did triple duty as an interrogation room and a break room, although Donny and Berta Ann rarely were anywhere but their desks in the bull pen behind the glass. He passed two holding cells, one of which held Val Broussard. She was curled up on the cot, and the idea of the small, vulnerable woman murdering anyone didn't make sense, except he'd seen her wallop the hell out of Berta Ann.

Ryder opened the break room door without knocking. Lance had his feet on the table, and a match three game held his attention on his phone. "Officer Kessler. Just the man I was hoping to see."

Kessler dropped his feet so fast that the chair wobbled dangerously. Ryder reached out a hand to steady it before the man landed on his ass. Although it would serve him right.

"Ryder. Didn't know you were here."

"Just stopped by for a visit. See if you've had any leads in the murder."

"Well, we've got the dead man's wife in a cell, so I'd say that's progress." He flashed a smile that belonged on a magazine cover.

Ryder lifted his brow. "She's the killer?"

"Sure seems that way to me."

"I guess you got a confession?"

"Oh no. I haven't questioned her. Not yet."

"Hmm." Ryder had plenty to say about that, but it wasn't his place.

"Uh. Just getting ready to, in fact. You want to sit in?" The officer popped out of his chair, ready to put on a show for Ryder. "Donny told me how much you helped out last summer, and—"

"Yep." No way he was leaving Kessler to question the woman who should have been questioned hours ago and released with a ticket or a summons or some such. "Has she been fed?"

"Oh. I'm not sure. You'd have to ask Berta Ann."

Ryder blinked at the man.

"Or I could. Yeah. I'll ask Berta Ann and then get Val and bring her in. Hang out here. Want a water?"

"Sure." The guy had seemed much more professional at the scene of the crime, but he'd had time to put on his game face. When Kessler was caught unawares, Ryder saw another side, and he didn't like it one bit. Donny better be learning a lot at that damn class, because he needed to get home and take care of business.

Lance returned with two bottles of water and a wilted Val. She sat at the table and drank a few sips. Ryder opened his bottle as well and waited. The untamed wild cat from that morning was a sad tabby, with hair flattened and clothes damp from the heat and lack of air circulation in the cell.

"Valerie Broussard, I'd like to review your rights with you." Lance rattled off the Miranda warning like a pro. "Are you willing to answer some questions?"

"I didn't kill my husband."

"Do you know who did?"

"No. I shouldn't have accused Henry." She traced a circle on the table with her chipped cherry-red fingernail. "I just don't know who could've, and I was angry."

"Henry?"

"Tank Murphy. The chef at Bay Leaves," Ryder supplied.

"My ex-husband," Val added.

"Had your ex-husband ever threatened Tony?"

"Not since our wedding three years ago. He told Tony he

better be good to me or there would be hell to pay. But that was just bluster. Henry couldn't hurt a fly."

"Was your husband insured? Life insurance?"

"Through his job. Nothing major—like fifty or sixty thousand, his base salary, I think. Not enough to even pay off our house." A tear tracked down her cheek. Ryder passed her a box of tissues from the bookcase behind him. "I was planning on leaving him anyway. I was just waiting until after the conference so it wouldn't be the big gossip. Guess I failed to dodge that bullet. Now that he's dead, I'm not sure what I'm going to do."

"Where were you Thursday night?"

"Me? I had a lot of organizing to do for the conference. Fix late registrations and fill in for no-show demonstrators. I had an evening review of the music lineup with the DJ."

"How late did that go?"

"Seven, I guess."

"What did you do afterward?"

"Went back to the trailer we have for the weekend to pack an overnight bag." She tapped her nails on the table. "Tony had a friend coming. But they'd already come and gone." Val gave Ryder a quick sideways glance. The behavioral tells said she was lying, but about what and why?

"Anyone see you? Or with you?"

"No." Tap, tap with the nails. There'd been a slight hesitation before she answered, too.

Officer Kessler kept going. "How did you know he'd been at the trailer?"

She sighed and crossed her arms. "The residue of coke on a mirror, the empty glasses next to the half-empty bottle of whiskey, and the smell of weed in the air."

"He used drugs regularly."

"Not around me. I don't tolerate it. But we have a sort of *what happens at conference stays at conference* agreement. Only I'd figured out a few months ago it wasn't just a conference blow-out thing. BDSM doesn't work well with mental impairment, so our sex life had pretty much died as well. And he was cheating."

"With who?"

"I don't know. That's why it was cheating. We have—*had*—an open marriage, but based on honesty. At least, it was supposed to be. We don't fuck others without a discussion first. Except at conference. Then he could yiff whoever."

"Furry sex," Kessler said. "Who did you stay with that night?"

Tap, tap. "Uh, Edwina Alman."

"When did you notice your husband was missing?"

"I... I didn't. As I said, we suspended our normal rules. We let ourselves be who we are sexually. No restrictions, except safe sex. I didn't know he was missing until that deputy found me at the community center and told me he was dead."

Lance had Berta Ann deliver the news? What the hell? Despite his namesake, so far, he appeared to be not too sharp and completely useless in the battle to find the killer.

"Who was your husband meeting that night?"

"He didn't say. I didn't ask." She crossed her arms. "How long are you going to keep me here?"

Lance glanced over at Ryder. After Ryder gave him nothing, he stood. "I need to check with the deputy. Ryder?"

They walked out together. Ryder stopped him in the hall. "You had Berta Ann notify?"

"Figured it would be easier coming from a woman."

What an asshole. "Find out anything on the murder weapon?"

"Blood on that leather matches the victim's blood. No usable prints."

"What about the sand?" If the crime scene techs took samples.

"Not from the beach. Too clean. They're running more tests."

"You're aware of the spanking demo the night before the

body was found. There was a tool used—leather dildo filled with sand?" Ryder so didn't want to have this conversation.

"I heard about that. In fact, Berta Ann brought it up when the preliminary findings came in."

"Did you ask her about—"

"She and Chuck went straight home. Couldn't have been either of them."

Was he stupid on purpose? "Did you confirm it was their tool that killed Tony?"

"No prints." Kessler gave him the same are-you-stupid look.

"We should ask."

Kessler nodded and strode down the hall.

Ryder followed the man into the bullpen.

"Berta Ann?" Lance asked. "Any reason we should keep Val in lockup?"

"Uh?" She ping-ponged her gaze from Kessler to Ryder and back. "I guess not. We can issue her a summons to appear for the assault, unless you're charging her with murder."

"We don't have enough evidence to make anything stick. Speaking of, that tool at your demo the night Broussard was killed—is yours missing?"

"I'm not sure. I'd have to check with Chuck. She takes care of that kind of thing." Berta Ann's face was bright red.

Ryder resisted the urge to squirm for her—discussing personal kinks in the workplace would make anyone uncomfortable, especially with a stranger.

"Okay. Then I think I'm going to release Mrs. Broussard but ask her to stick around in town."

Berta Ann nodded and returned her attention to the computer.

Ryder clapped Lance on the shoulder. "You've got things under control here. I've got some things to take care of."

Val's alibi—meeting with DJ Damon—would be easy enough to check. Not that lazy Officer Kessler would bother. Ryder searched the obvious places for Damon's van to find out if he'd really met with Valerie and how late the meeting went. He hit pay dirt near the river on the edge of town at the Pink Petals strip club. The van was parked in the back lot. Inside, the bar was dim, the main stage unlit with a single pole occupying the empty stage. Table and chairs hugged the platform, waiting for patrons to arrive. Ryder threaded his way stage left and found the skinny blond twenty-something fussing with wires in the DJ booth.

"Damon?"

Damon, or "DJ Slick" as he preferred, sprang up, banging his head on the counter with the two turntable decks.

"Hey, Ryder, what can I do for you?" He rubbed his head over his lanky hair, blinking back the moisture in his eyes.

"You're the DJ for the conference?"

"Yeah. It's killing me, moving the equipment back and forth, messing with these cables. But Olive's been getting big crowds, and tonight will be huge. After this conference is over, I'm sleeping for three days. I swear."

"You met with the lady running Cowbells on Thursday?"

"Val. Yeah. She's cool, but, like, kind of uptight. Wanted to review all the songs for the dance competition that night and the fashion show the next day."

"What time did you meet?"

"Don't know. After she got back from the Tool Shed and before the dance competition, so five?"

Ryder would have to check the schedule. "And how long did it take you to go over everything?"

"Couple hours. Felt like longer."

"Did you go to the demo at the Tool Shed?"

"Nah, me and Caleb were moving all the equipment. Caleb picked up a few bucks helping the decorators with all the pipe and drape."

"What time did the contest start?"

"Seven thirty. People started showing up earlier, getting into costume."

"Did Mrs. Broussard stay for the dance competition?"

"Not the whole thing. Left before her tiger performed." Damon crossed his arms and gave a smug half smile. "The chief was waiting for her. Hovering near the exit."

"Frank?"

"Yep. He was trying to be all casual but practically ran after her when she stormed out. Not sure what set her off, but she knew Chief was there." Damon smirked. "Mike could probably tell you more. She was backstage when whatever set Val off happened. Alls I know is I got a last-minute change, and Tony, Val's husband, had a solo when he should have been part of the 'Oh My' dance group."

"Oh My?"

"Yeah, guess they started out with a lion, a tiger, and a bear. But it's been an elephant, tiger, and bear the last few years."

"Anything else you can remember? Especially about the tiger?"

"Just that his crew was pissed when he won the solo competition and they lost for the group. Pretty sure the bear told him 'You're dead to me,' but it was kind of loud in there with all the cheering. Especially Letty and Shelly. Jeez, those women are screamers."

Ryder filed that detail into things he wished he didn't know. He glanced at his watch. Mike would be done at the salon soon. "Thanks, D. I'll let you know if I have more questions."

"Sure, man. See you tonight."

Ryder nodded as he left. Parked in front of the Root Zone, he turned over the facts and possibilities. The tiger had been alive after the demo—likely killed with Chuck's dildo sometime later that night. Val was planning to divorce the guy, and she probably was fucking around with Frank. Tiger's buddies were pissed that he'd ditched them for the dance competition. There were limp motivations and weak alibis, but nothing stood out, except that he should have Officer Kessler track down an elephant and a bear. He pulled up the number but called Berta Ann instead. She'd do a better job. As soon as he was done with the call, he got out of the truck to get some air. Hot for October, but better than sitting inside the closed-up cab.

The door opened, and Mike took his breath. Her dark-brown hair had been woven into braids that started at the crown of her head and twisted around, completely pinned up. Her red nails flashed in the late afternoon sun. Sophisticated and perfectly put together. How soon could he have her dragging those nails down his back while he freed that twist and tugged her hair loose, disassembling her into the wild wanton woman he craved? He moved to the lowest step. "Need a lift, gorgeous?"

A slow, sweet smile lifted the corners of her luscious lips. "Sure, handsome. Where have *you* been?"

"Doing a bit of sleuthing."

"Learn anything?"

"Later. We have a party to go to." He gripped her hips and gave her a chaste kiss while she was at the perfect height. There would be so much more, but later. Ryder guided her down the stairs and opened the passenger door. She already looked hot as hell, but he couldn't wait to see her in the outfit he'd bought for the Ring My Bell night at the Pink Petals. She was going to set the place on fire.

CHAPTER NINE

At his insistence, Mike led the way up the stairs from the garage to Ryder's apartment. "You just want to stare at my ass."

"Yep." His low voice washed over her, and she shivered with anticipation. His hand went to her back. "Don't fall."

As if he would let her. She opened the door and was instantly attacked. A black ball of fur launched into the air, landing in her arms. "Mow. Hi, baby. Miss me?"

Ryder's three-legged rescue cat, who hated everyone, purred in her arms and rubbed her head against Mike's chest.

"She thinks you should move in too," Ryder said as he walked past them to the bedroom. "We should get changed. Gonna grab a quick shower. There's food in the fridge. Help yourself."

"Thank god. I'm starved. Has Mow been fed?"

"Her feeder should have plenty of kibble."

Mike checked the automated dispenser, and sure enough, it was loaded. She placed Mow on the ground and retrieved the cat's covert treat container from the cabinet. Mow serpentined through Mike's legs, purring and rubbing against them.

"Yes, of course you're going to get a treat." She handed over the first soft nugget. "But don't tell your dad. He thinks I spoil you." Mike gave Mow a second chew and hid the canister again. It was Mike and Mow's secret game. Well, as secret as anyone could get with that man.

"Mow get her treats?" He stood in the doorway of his bedroom, water beading down his chest to the towel wrapped around his hips.

She licked her lips. "What?"

He laughed. "Come back here. Let's get you dressed."

She crossed to him as he turned his back and took his towel off to dry his hair.

"Jeezus." The man's ass should come with a warning.

"Need something?" Ryder's deep voice rumbled through her.

Yeah, about three hours alone with him. "We should hurry. Don't want to be late."

With a devious grin, he spun and pressed her to the wall, kissing her neck, her arms lifted over her head. His mouth connected with hers, and time stopped. His kisses were a drug, and when he pulled away to guide her shirt over her head, she missed his heat, his taste, the sweet pressure of his lips against hers. But he was back on her in a moment, nibbling at her neck, as if he was just as hungry for her.

Fuck the Petals.

She already had enough material to write up. They could go to bed and make love all night. He slipped her bra off her arms. When had he undone the clasp? When had he released her? Didn't matter since he was sliding his strong hands down her thighs and dragging her jeans and panties in one continuous move.

She let him finish getting her completely naked. His body covered hers—his erection pressed tightly between them. She rocked her hips and rolled her spine, searching for their connection. He moved his hand between her legs and stroked his fingers across her pussy. She'd beg if he stopped kissing her long enough. The ache inside built, demanding his cock. She slid her leg up his thigh to wrap around him, and finally he pressed his finger into her. The single digit teased instead of satisfying her. He brushed her clit but didn't give her the touch he knew would set her off.

Fuck.

She ripped her lips from his. "Please."

He took two steps back. Naked, hard Ryder. She lunged at him, but he dodged. "Later, M. We've got to go."

Her mouth fell open when he held out the shopping bag to her. "You did that on purpose."

"Maybe." But his half smile and the gleam in his eye told her everything. He'd edged her.

She dropped to her knees, grabbed his cock, and sucked him to the back of her throat before he could move. His taste so familiar and sensual. She cupped his balls firmly in her other hand. With an ease from taking him repeatedly in the past months, she sucked him in and out, deeper and deeper. When he thrust his hips to her rhythm, she released him from her mouth and dropped her hands, rising to her feet. She grinned. "Okay, I think we're ready to get dressed now."

"You're wicked," Ryder groaned. "We have to make an appearance at the Petals. I promised Olive." He lifted a single brow. "After, I'm taking advantage of you all night long."

"Deal." But it would be at her place because she had articles to write first thing in the morning.

"I got you something." He pulled a hanger from his closet. A black minidress hung from it. "I'll help you get into it."

"You bought me a dress?" He'd said he was buying her an outfit, but she didn't expect a dress. A sexy one too, with a collar and strips of fabric down to a bandeau top and more strips to a miniskirt. It looked sexy as fuck on the hanger. Could she pull it off? "What about shoes?"

"Got you covered." He draped the dress over the end of the

bed. Another quick trip to the closet, and he held up a pair of Grecian-style sandals, also black. And flat.

"Perfect." She slid the dress from the hanger and undid the hook-and-eyes at the collar and top. The stretchy skirt would fit like a second skin. "What should I wear under this?"

He opened the top drawer of his dresser that held the few items she kept at his place and twirled a scrap of black around his finger. "These."

With her free hand, she snatched the thong from his hand. "Seriously?"

He took them back and dropped to one knee, holding them open. "Step in."

His cock was still hard as hell. She gripped his bare shoulder. Getting dressed in anything was a terrible plan but having him dress her was total seduction. She placed each foot carefully through the leg hole and he slid them up her thighs, teasing her heated skin the entire way. As the fabric covered her pussy, her core clenched, wet and hot. He took his time adjusting the thong perfectly over her ass and hips. Each graze of his fingers another electric tease.

"Now for the dress."

They repeated the same game. He adjusted the skirt perfectly and took his time to smooth each thread of fabric over her ass. It might be October, but it was hot as July in that bedroom. He rose from the ground, leaving the top of the dress folded forward over the front of the skirt. He cupped each of her naked breasts in a hand and raised them alternately to his mouth, sucking, licking, and giving her a tender nip. Electricity shot through her.

"Perfect," he said as he playfully pinched each nipple.

Mike was going to come and the panties would be pointless, but no way would she tell him to stop. What event?

He circled behind her and lifted the front of the dress, capturing her taut breasts in the fabric and clipping it closed at her back. He took his time to adjust her inside the bandeau, his erection pressed to her ass. Mike dropped her head back to his shoulder. He really should reverse all of this—strip her naked—and fuck the hell out of her. But this was his game, and she loved it when he took control. In the bedroom.

He nipped her neck, and she straightened. "Hey."

Ryder chuckled as he fitted the collar of the dress around her neck and clipped it closed. Mike's pussy was vibrating with need. Her chest ached, and shivers ran down her spine. She reached back and stroked Ryder's cock. "Sure we have to go?"

He slid out of her grasp. "We do."

Mike huffed. "Fine."

"Don't worry. I'll take care of you later. Promise."

"I'm holding you to that." She sat on the bed and slipped on one sandal, grateful they closed with a zipper along the back and that she didn't have to figure out all the crisscrossing laces.

He dressed in his black jeans and boots but with a black button-down shirt open enough to see the hint of the compass rose tattoo over his heart. Mike slicked on a vibrant red lipstick and a few swipes of mascara. She got a little light-headed as he rolled the sleeves of his shirt. What was the deal with the man's forearms?

"Come on." He held out his hand to her. "We're already late."

CALEB, the beefy bouncer, read a book while perched on a stool in the vestibule of the Pink Petals entrance. The cover was a desert vista with a blue sky and *Warrior* in the title.

"This one any good?" Mike asked.

He raised his clean-shaven chin, his mop of sandy hair falling in his eyes. "Superb. It's a mystery set in New Mexico with a hint of romance and pretty spooky."

"I get to borrow it when you're done."

Caleb nodded, and Ryder led them inside the strip club.

Olive had remodeled after she'd gotten full ownership of the place last summer. She'd elevated the vibe with fresh coats of charcoal-gray paint and accents of neon-blue lights along the edge of the stage and the back wall. All the seating had been upgraded too, new vinyl in dark blue and faux marble tabletops. Mike asked if they were real the first time she saw them, and Olive laughed. They still looked real to Mike. The houseboat bar, skirting the county liquor laws by floating beyond the state line, was attached to the main structure with a wide framed opening that made it difficult to tell where the boat began. The new bar top matched the faux marble tables. And blue lights accented the mirror behind the liquor shelves.

Mike followed Ryder through the club, stopping at the only unoccupied martini table, its top covered in a black cloth and tied with a blue piece of fabric around the base. On the spot-lighted stage apron, a man was tying intricate knots around his sub's barely clad body with black ropes hung from a length of bamboo suspended from the ceiling. An eighties song about a stalker watching the target's every breath filled the background. People thought it was a love song. Mike thought it was creepy, but it had a good beat. The sub's golden flesh filled the gaps in the ropes, emphasizing the restraints. As the song came to a close, the man pulled two ropes in a way that suspended the sub in midair. Mike gasped along with the audience. The rigger slowly spun his bound sub through space. It was oddly beautiful, but not the least bit sexually enticing.

Ryder finally turned from the bar with two yellow labeled Texas beers in his hand. She stared at him like the stalker in the song as he sauntered back. If he ever dressed up in a fursuit, not that he ever would, he'd have to be a panther. He set the beers down, and she downed a mouthful of the frosty brew as she glanced around. No one was in a furry costume. The prevailing color was black, mostly leather, lots of metal. There were a few familiar faces, including Albert and Kenny, the Elephant and Bear, in street clothes, sitting close to the stage. The audience broke out into applause as the freed sub and the rigger left the stage.

The lights lowered, even the accent lighting. DJ Slick announced the next scene. Fire Chief Frank appeared on stage shirtless, rolling out what looked like a massage table. He draped it in a cloth then held out his hand. The entire room remained silent as he led a silhouetted woman to the table. He assisted her as she maneuvered herself facedown. Then he slid the short kimono style robe from her shoulders. She was completely bare from what little Mike could see.

Another woman, one Mike recognized as a regular Pink Petals dancer, entered the stage with a cart filled with equipment. Fire wands, like the ones he'd used on Mike during the demo at the station, were arranged in a glass vase like two dozen white roses.

"Attendees, for your safety, please remain seated during the scene," DJ Slick stated in a subdued and authoritarian tone. Mike was impressed he could pull it off. "We will dim the lights completely so that you can enjoy the artistry."

Electronic dance music with a heavy rhythmic beat started, and the entire club went pitch black for a few seconds before the first burst of flame danced across the woman's back in a circular pattern. Frank wasn't lighting the wands this time. He drew on her body with the fuel and then lit it, wiping away the flame with his hand. Only their skin—his hands, her back—was illuminated. The flames danced to the music. The pictures lasted seconds. The beauty spoke to a primal part of Mike's brain that equated fire with life.

Frank's submissive shifted on the table in a sensuous undulation, only the merest glimpses of her naked body visible and always with the chief's hand gliding across her.

Mike had no idea how long the dance had been going on when Olive's voice drew her attention back to the table.

"Ryder, I've got a minor problem with the lineup," Olive whispered.

"What's up?" Ryder asked so low his voice was merely a vibration.

"Tony and Val were supposed to do an impact scene. Frank was supposed to be using Shayna, my dancer, as his partner. But now everything is out of whack. Tony's not— I don't have a scene to bring people back from this part of the night. You know I can't leave them in this fire trance."

Mike didn't know what Olive was talking about. Was a fire trance even a thing, or was she just trying to get Ryder on stage?

"Can you and Mike fill in?"

"What?" Mike hissed. Impact? Nope. What the hell was Olive thinking?

Headline: Writer Whipped by White-Hot Lover

Mike squirmed in her seat.

"I can do it," Ryder said, "but Mike doesn't want to go up. You got someone else I can play with?"

"Hell no." Mike bristled. Two seconds earlier, the worst idea had been going up on the stage. Ryder fixed that. No way was he doing a scene with someone else. But she couldn't leave Olive hanging either. "I'll do it."

"Great. Let's get you backstage." Olive had a low-light flashlight that she pointed at the floor as she guided them away from the bar and Mike's beer and her brains.

The music on stage crescendoed, and the flames licked all over Val's body as Mike and Ryder went through the backstage door and into the lighted dressing room.

"I have some tools you can choose from. Just put them on the teacart, and Chandra will wheel them out for you. We'll have a short break while we get the St. Andrews cross on stage.

I'll announce the regatta parade winner, and then I'll introduce you."

Cross?

Mike gulped.

What had she agreed to?

Ryder picked up a wand with feathers at the end. Feathers? Okay, so the impact wouldn't be a big deal. And she was used to him slapping her ass during sex. Looked forward to it. Then he picked up a wand with a leather heart on the end. That...might leave a mark. Next, he selected a long thick piece of leather with a handle. The tray was starting to look like one of the BDSM vendor booths back at the community center.

"I have to pee." Mike had no desire to continue to monitor Ryder's selections. And it wasn't like she could back out at this point. She darted out of the dressing room and back up the hall to the women's restrooms. As soon as the swinging door shut, voices filled the hallway.

"Calm down." She recognized Frank McCready's voice.

"I shouldn't have done the scene with you." It was Val Broussard. "What will people think? Tony just died. Was killed. Murdered. And I'm up on stage playing with my lover. Did you know Ryder Ruiz was at the station when they questioned me?"

"What?"

Mike pressed her ear to the edge of the door while holding the handle so it didn't fly open.

"Yeah, and I found out he's dating the reporter for the newspaper. I have a real life and a job, Frank. An article in a paper could get picked up. Go viral."

"You're getting all worked up. How about some chocolate and a cuddle?"

"This isn't fucking sub drop. It's going to be hard enough telling people Tony died while we were on vacation. What if the Dallas news reprints that fucking article?"

"That's not going to happen."

"You don't know that." The sound of a smack accompanied Val's words. "I can't even leave early because that cop told me to stay in town. Fucking Tony. That man fucked up everything he touched. I should have just left him months ago."

"You know I'm here for you Val, baby."

"Don't 'baby' me. I need to go."

"I'll come with you."

"No. You won't. We're done. I can't risk an affair going public during all of this, too."

Mike snorted softly. The affair was common knowledge—and not the first, from what she'd heard. Who did this woman think she was fooling?

"You can't drive home in a robe."

"Give me my bag. I'll get changed in there."

Mike darted back to the last stall and closed the door, trying to control her breathing as Val stomped into the bathroom. What would she do if she discovered Mike hiding? But it was too late to just use the toilet like she hadn't been eavesdropping.

How damn long did it take for a woman to put on underwear, jeans, and a t-shirt? She must have been doing her full makeup. If Mike didn't get out of there soon, Ryder would come looking for her. Water in the sink ran for a minute. Mike squirmed with the reminder she still hadn't emptied her nervous bladder. The click of heels and squeak of the door had Mike breathing again. She put her feet on the floor and lifted the lid to the toilet.

As soon as she stepped out of the restroom, she ran into Ryder.

"You okay?" His eyebrows were pinched together as he inspected her.

"Just nerves. I'm fine now."

"Good. They're waiting for us." He tugged her hand, and they entered the stage as DJ Slick announced her and Ryder.

"Breathe." Ryder locked his gaze to hers. "It stops any time you want. 'Stop.' 'No.' 'I'm done.' You say the word, any word, and I'll end the scene immediately. You're in control, M."

She nodded and let him guide her to a big wooden X on stage.

"I'm going to cuff you."

She lifted her shaking right arm for him. And then her left. He went to his knees. But instead of latching her onto the X as she expected...he attached a bar to her ankles, spreading her feet apart.

CHAPTER TEN

A SHIVER ROSE FROM WHERE RYDER'S HANDS WERE ON HER ankles. He trailed his fingers around the spreader bar clamps to the outside of her legs, leaving heat and need in his wake. His touch stuttered against the straps of her sandals. As he rose, his bare chest brushed against her, intimate and connected. When had he taken his shirt off? Backstage? She hadn't noticed, too concerned about what would happen on stage. In front of an audience she couldn't see, but they were there, eyes boring into her.

He gripped the interlaced braids in her hair and turned her head so that she met his eyes. His beautiful face filled her field of view. His breath tickled her ear. "With me?"

She nodded as much as his hold allowed.

"Words."

"Yes," she panted.

His lips briefly met hers before he released her and took a step back. Before she could miss his touch, he danced his fingers up from her hips to the clasps of the collar on her dress and released them. The bandeau quickly followed. Except the fabric didn't drop. Ryder quickly fixed it, pulling her top down, baring her back to the audience. Naked from the waist up in a crowded room—it should have made her scared or nervous. Instead, she arched into Ryder's touch when he traced his fingers down her spine.

A collective sigh filled the room.

Yeah, her man was hot as hell, and everyone in the club knew it.

A tickling sensation ran along her neck. Ryder must've grabbed the feather wand when she'd been focused on the audience. With that first caress, nobody else existed but him.

The feathers woke every nerve as he trailed them over her sensitive skin. He retraced each area where she reacted, intensifying her awareness of her own skin to a new height, along with her arousal. When he slid the feathers between her spread thighs and across the gusset of her panties, she could have sworn he'd stolen the tiny scrap he'd dressed her in earlier. Every muscle inside her clenched, begging for release.

Ryder smacked her ass over her skirt with his bare hand. Each side. Repeatedly. The sting layered on top of the soft tease of the feathers fired unfamiliar areas of her brain. The ache in her pussy multiplied. Then he stopped. But not for long.

Leather hit high on the outside of her thigh, branding heat across her flesh. She swallowed back a squeal. Her skirt bunched up to just below her ass. Ryder serpentined around her, dropping stinging slaps that she was sure were leaving heart-shaped red marks all over her exposed body. Shoulder, upper arm, inner thigh. A drag of the leather. The wand disappearing from her skin, only to snap against her in a fresh spot. Pain shattering into pleasure with each strike. Patterns rose as he painted marks on her like an artist and she transformed to simple fabric on a frame.

"How are you doing, M?"

His voice brought her back to being Mike instead of a canvas. She searched for a word. "Good."

"Keep going?"

"Yes, please." She wasn't ready to stop exploring what Ryder could do to her.

Instead of words, he caressed her body with his hands to signal his approval. Her muscles softened under his care. But only for a moment before a cascade of slight stings covered an area as big as his hand. He'd exchanged the heart-shaped leather crop for a new toy. Over and over again, moving in a rhythmic dance, the small flogger increased the heat across her entire body. The effect was similar to the feather but more intense. Her sense of awareness lifted above her body, floating, and she relaxed into the sensation.

Ryder paused, but she was only aware of it peripherally because her body still sang with the stimulation. *Smack.*

"Oh." Mike stiffened, tugged from her feathery fog.

Smack.

Damn. That wasn't the flogger. The nerves in her body whipped at her with the change in intensity. The pain pooled in her nipples and her clit.

Smack.

Holy shit. The blow was lower, just below her ass. Her eyes watered.

"One more, M."

Seriously?

Smack.

She cried out as the cascade of sensation sent her spiraling. A distant crash rattled the metal of the tea cart, and Ryder was against her. His bare chest against her sensitive back and his jeans pressing into her screaming bottom.

"So good," he whispered. "You did so well."

His praise washed over her, soothing, cleansing. He kissed her neck as he redressed her. Rubbed her ass with one hand as he released the tether on her left arm then freed her right.

"Hold on right here, M." He positioned her hands on the

middle of the X and dropped low behind her. The bar separating her legs clattered onto the cart, and then he swooped her into his arms and carried her backstage, the noise of the audience quickly fading. The scent of motors, musk, and rain—Ryder—comforted Mike as she pressed her face to his neck.

Instead of the strippers' dressing room, they went into Olive's plush, headliner-worthy retreat. The lighting was dim, and Ryder sat with her on his lap, surrounded by the white wood cabinets that held Olive's costumes. He draped a soft blanket over her and held a water bottle to her lips. After a few sips and a couple bites of chocolate, Mike wriggled in his hold.

"What do you need, M?"

"I should be writing. And I'm starving."

Ryder's chest shook with silent laughter. "I'll feed you. But you're coming home with me. Because if you think after that I won't fuck you until dawn, you're mistaken."

Mike's pussy clenched in agreement. Stupid body. She had a deadline. "My place, so I can write in the morning."

"We'll get your laptop and anything else you need. My bed's bigger."

She could continue to argue, but it would only delay getting food. "Fine. But—"

He held up his phone. "I'm already calling in an order."

At her place, she stuffed her laptop and notebooks in the satchel, along with a clean pair of panties and her favorite writing pajamas and slippers, while Ryder picked up the burgers and fries from Jerry's. The lights from his truck lit up her dark hallway. She glanced at the bookcase. An odd sensation of forgetting something lingered at the back of her brain, but Ryder had delivered the cake topper. Locking up, she rushed to the truck so she could stuff her face with hot greasy potatoes on the short drive to his shop.

RYDER CARRIED Mike's computer bag up the stairs to the entrance of his loft apartment. The place was perfect—for him —with its twelve-stair commute to his work, nestled in the outskirts of town. Only one problem—Mike wouldn't agree to live there. But that didn't matter because she was right behind him on the stairway, still nibbling fries out of the bags from Jerry's. Good thing he'd had Jorge include a large order. Even better that she'd agreed to stay tonight, because after he fed her, he was going to put that body to use. It had been a long time since he'd done a scene with anyone. He winced at the flash of the last time, mostly due to the person he'd played with. That had been a goat rodeo in the end. But Mike had nothing in common with his ex-boss.

The control Mike had given Ryder earlier—the trust—startled him. The entire time, at least after the feather wand, he'd expected her to tap out. Instead, she'd gone deeper with him, to the point he'd been bold enough to use the paddle. Even then, she hadn't asked to stop—but her cry was enough. She wasn't used to that kind of play. In fact, he should have spent more time talking to her before they ever went up on stage. But he'd become so comfortable with her and her boundaries. At times, it felt like they were of one mind. The only contention between them was living together—and that was just a matter of time.

They finished their burgers in moments. He threw away the wrappers and schemed about how to get them back in the right mood.

"I heard Val and Frank talking in the hall before we went on stage." Pink tinged Mike's cheeks.

Was she blushing because of what she heard or what they'd done? Ryder suspected the latter.

"She was the one on stage with him, during the fire play."

Ryder grunted his acknowledgement. Seemed a bit insensitive with her husband in the morgue.

"Apparently, she was thinking of leaving Tony. I guess she

and the chief have been *dating* for a while. She was worried that I might find out because you were at the police station during her interrogation and I'm a reporter."

"You're not reporting on the murder."

"I know. But the dang thing needs to get cleared up. Heather's wedding is going to be a disaster if there's still an active crime scene just beyond the tents."

"You know nothing will *ruin* her wedding if she really loves Jason. The only thing that matters is that the two people who are in love are there and willing to commit their lives to each other. Willing to face any adversity, celebrate every win, together. Everything else is extra. So if the situation isn't perfect on the day of the event, it really doesn't matter because life goes on. And Heather knows you're doing your best. Hell, you've basically acted as her on-site wedding coordinator."

Mike tugged at the collar of her dress. "I know. But solving the murder before next weekend would be—"

"I asked Lance to look into Tony's dance crew. One of them could have been pissed off enough with him, I guess. I don't think Val could have done it. Maybe the first blow, but not the rest."

"So you think she may know who did it?"

Ryder shrugged. "I'm sure she has her suspicions, but she's not sharing them."

"What about Frank? I can't see him doing it, but he's dating her and obviously they have an intense relationship based on their scene."

"You liked the fire performance?" Ryder held his face in a neutral mask, not letting Mike see what he really thought and how unhappy he was that the chief had used her for the demo.

"Yeah, I liked it. It was hot. I mean, duh, fire. But seriously, their connection on stage and the sensuousness of him setting her on fire and putting it out. It was sexy as hell."

"You want to play with fire?"

Mow hopped up in Mike's lap and demanded attention. She paused, petting the silky black cat. "Not really. It was fun in a risky, try-this-once kind of way. But I'm so damn accident prone, it's a terrible idea to get into it as a regular thing. Plus, it didn't turn me on near as much as you running a feather over me. Or a flogger."

"How about the crop?"

She blinked up at him. "Yeah. I liked that, too."

"Let me see."

"What?"

"Stand up. I want to see if my marks are still there." And make sure he hadn't injured her with his enthusiasm.

"*Your* marks, huh?" She placed Mow on the ground, stood, and faced away.

Faint heart-shaped outlines barely showed on her shoulders and lower thighs. Ryder traced over the evidence of her trust with the lightest of touch and breathed a sigh of relief. He hadn't bruised her. At least not with the crop. But he should check the areas he'd paddled and marked her as his. He should check her entire body. His cock woke up, demanding. "Go into the bedroom and strip. Facedown on the bed."

Mike spun around and gave him a smirk. She released the hooks on her dress and shimmied it over her hips on the way to his room. By the time she disappeared, she was wearing only the thong, her sandals, and the red splotches she'd allowed him to paint all over her. Ryder adjusted his cock and tried to count to one hundred. At fifty-two, he bee-lined for the door that hid Mike from his view.

CHAPTER ELEVEN

MIKE HURRIED TO RELEASE THE ZIPPERS ON HER SHOES AND tucked them into the closet. She ditched her panties in the hamper and flopped facedown on the bed with no idea how long it would be before Ryder came in. The exhaustion that had been teasing her after three long days of covering the convention and searching for a killer faded at the anticipation of more of Ryder's command games. The actual scene they'd done at the club played on rewind, the details sparking through her like being there again. He'd done those things before, with someone else. But she wasn't jealous, more surprised—at herself, and him. Impact play turned him on based on the erection he'd had on stage and his need to inspect "his marks." Because he required control, or at least the appearance of control?

Before she could decide what to do with this new Ryder insight, the bedroom door clicked shut.

Her man was there, behind her. Mike's nipples hardened with anticipation and the unknown.

What would the newly unleashed Ryder want to do in the privacy of his bedroom with no onlookers? He'd kept her nudity to a minimum on stage, her bare breasts hidden from the audience.

That wasn't an issue anymore, lying on his bed stark naked while his eyes roamed over her, their path heated her as if he was actually touching. His fingers grazed over her ass, and she jumped. Damn, he moved so silently.

"Nervous?"

"Excited," she responded.

"Good." He lowered himself onto the bed next to her. He was as bare as she was. *Yes.* There could never be enough naked-Ryder minutes in the day. He gently tugged her hair free of the twist and braids Shelly had so carefully crafted, massaging Mike's scalp as he released the tension.

She moaned and melted into the bed a little more.

"You were beautiful tonight." Ryder traced one of the still sensitive heart marks with his finger.

"I didn't know that was something you liked."

"Once upon a time, I belonged to a club."

"Something you want to get back into?" Mike wasn't sure what she'd say if he said yes. Or no.

Ryder peppered kisses down her back and nipped her ass. "The only place I want to 'get back into' is you."

He really hadn't answered the question. But maybe he didn't have an answer, and not everything had to be decided that night. Especially when he was running his hands all over her body, squeezing the tender spots at the tops of her thighs.

"Was I too hard on you?"

"No, but I wouldn't mind you being hard on me now." She flipped her hair back and met his gaze over her shoulder, waggling her eyebrows.

Ryder chuckled. "Roll over, M."

She shifted, and he gripped her breasts then ran his hands down her sides. He lifted her leg at the knee and tugged her to the edge of the bed before sliding off and positioning himself on the floor with his face cradled in between her legs.

"I'm going to make you come so hard. And then I'm going to fuck you so deep into that mattress you'll never want to leave."

Before Mike could respond to his roundabout way of demanding she live with him, again, he slid two fingers into her already aroused pussy and lapped at her with his tongue, teasing her clit with the tip.

Her mouth and brain forgot words. There were none for the tension coiling low and deep. The orgasm that had been sitting on the sidelines, the one that had built during their scene, roared to the forefront. There was no stopping the storm that crashed through her, locking every muscle in a taut pose of pleasure before the flood released. She shook as Ryder guided her through every diminishing aftershock.

After she went boneless, Ryder kissed her thighs then rose. His thick cock strained toward her, and if she had muscles left, she would have reached for him. He flipped her over. She attempted to move up the bed, but his hand landed on her ass with a smack that went right to her wrecked pussy. She writhed with the ache of emptiness.

"Don't move." The nightstand drawer snapped closed. Ryder always remembered a condom. He lifted her hips and thrust so deep inside her, she gasped for breath. Two more hard pulses, and his balls slapped her clit.

"Holy shit." Mike dug her fingers into the covers and held on.

Ryder's grip on her hips tightened. He slid out, only to jackhammer back in.

Mike released an incoherent collection of syllables begging for more, deeper, yes, please. Thankfully, Ryder spoke orgasmic Mike, and he translated her requests perfectly, pounding into her fast and hard, taking her up and up to the edge she'd become so familiar with.

"Ryder," she called his name as she tumbled over into free-floating ecstasy and spasmed around his hard cock. He continued to work her until she finally returned to her body. As soon as she settled, he jerked his hips twice more before losing his pace with a roar. Mike pushed her hips back to give him more, of her, of their sex, of anything she could.

He collapsed over her, his hot, heavy weight cementing their connection. Then he rolled them over, keeping his still-hard cock inside, both of them panting for air.

"How do you do that?" Mike asked.

"I was going to ask you the same thing. You wreck me." He clutched her closer.

It was the same for her. There would never be another man who connected with her so well, understood her without questions, and catered to her idiosyncrasies rather than criticized them.

Headline: Reporter Ruined by Warrior's Wanton Rides

She let herself relax into his hold.

RYDER WOKE FROM A DEEP SLEEP. He never slept so fully except when Mike stayed over, but she wasn't in the bed. A rattle in the kitchen put a smile on his face. He slipped on a pair of sleep pants and went to find out what she was attempting to create in his kitchen.

"Are you *cooking?*"

Mike squealed, and the jar of mayonnaise went flying out of her hands. Ryder snagged the glass out of the air before it hit the floor.

"You scared the crap out of me."

He set the jar on the counter next to the loaf of bread. "Make me one, too?"

"Yep." The toaster dinged, and she loaded two more slices of bread.

Retreating to the small table, he savored the domestic moment. Not that Mike was any more domesticated than him, but it was nice being up in the middle of the night, sharing a snack. Nice that she felt comfortable enough in his space to treat it as her own. Nice that he didn't wake up in the middle of the night because she wasn't in his bed. Well, he had, but at least she was in his kitchen, not across town.

"You should move in with me." Ryder regretted the words the moment they escaped his lips.

She stiffened but continued to pile meat and cheese on the toast before cutting the sandwiches in half. After dropping the knife in the sink and tucking away the perishables, she brought their plates to the table. They ate silently. Ryder couldn't retrieve the words, so he waited for her response.

"Why? Why is this such a big deal?" Mike asked before picking up the second half of her sandwich.

"I worry about you. I wake up in the middle of the night, and I imagine you're in some danger. I've even driven by your place to make sure you're okay so I can sleep." She'd likely freak out if she knew how often he performed those security patrols.

"I'm sorry you can't sleep, but that's your paranoia. I'm fine. I write community news in a tiny little town."

"Where the wives of murdered men worry about the story you're going to write."

She finished chewing. "The cameras you installed at the office are good."

"I'm too many minutes away to *prevent* anything from happening." Their argument from the past weeks was on repeat.

"I can't let fear drive my life."

"Isn't it fear that's keeping you from moving in? Fear we won't work out? Fear that you'd be giving up everything?"

"So you have been listening."

"To every word. But you haven't changed my mind."

"And you haven't changed mine. There's no room for me here. It's your shop and your closet and your kitchen. Besides that, people stop by all the time. When would I be able to get in the zone and write? And where? *Your* office?"

"You'd still be working at the *Peat*. You'd still have an office."

She picked up their empty plates and washed up.

Ryder mulled over what she'd said. Not only the words, but the possible issues behind them. There had to be a way to make this work. "I—" He choked on the word he wasn't sure she was ready to hear. "I want to be with you, M."

She shut off the water and wiped her hands. Then she went to him and sat in his lap. "I want to be with you, too, Ryder. I *am* with you."

Her kisses confirmed she wasn't lying, and he wrapped his arms around her before taking her back to bed. The bed she should sleep in every night. And would eventually, because he wasn't giving up. Mike snuggled into him, using his arm for a pillow, and he returned to the deep sleep he only got when she stayed over.

The sharp sound of a phone had Ryder on instant alert, but it wasn't his. "M. Your phone."

She blinked at him and swiped at her eyes. "What time is it?"

"Not sure." He got out of bed and found it in the kitchen. Edwina. Why would she be calling? Ryder answered the call and told her to hold on. "Here." He held the cell out to Mike.

She lifted it to her ear. "Hello?"

Ryder could hear the Town Council Chair's shrill voice as if his own ear were on the phone. "*The Daily Peat* is on fire. Where are you?"

"What?" Mike flung back the covers.

"Mikaela Mitchell. The office is on fire. Did you leave the stove on?"

"What do you mean, 'on fire?' I don't cook."

"The fire department is trying to put it out, but the structure is probably going to be a total loss."

"No—"

"You should be here." Weenie's imperious tone grated on Ryder's last nerve. Not one word of condolence or relief that Mike was safe.

The call ended. Mike set her phone on the nightstand. She wobbled to her feet and tugged her hair, her gaze darting around the room. "I need to... I need to get dressed."

Mike retreated to the bathroom. Ryder went to the kitchen. Coffee—Mike was in shock. His neck tightened with a sense of foreboding. Someone had set Mike's office on fire. He had no evidence, but he was sure of it.

And, likely, they'd thought she was inside. Thank God he'd insisted she stay at his place. What if she'd refused? Been alone? He set his jaw. His stomach churned as a flash from his military past reminded just how gruesome fire could be.

Ryder leaned over the sink and threw up his sandwich from earlier.

The killer had come after his woman. He rinsed his mouth and sent everything down the disposal. Once he had the coffee brewing, he'd come up with a plan to keep Mike safe and catch the killer.

CHAPTER TWELVE

Mike got out of Ryder's truck to assess the damage to her office and her home as the sun begun to rise. A half dozen volunteer firefighters, sweaty and sooty, lingered around what was left of the structure. The front porch seemed untouched, if you didn't notice the front door was missing. Holes gaped in the roof. Scorch marks marred the exterior walls. All that remained beyond, inside her home, appeared to be charcoal. *A total loss.* Weenie's word from the call earlier rattled though Mike's chest. Tears welled in her eyes.

"Chief," Ryder said.

Mike turned from the devastation.

"Ryder. Mike," Frank said. "I'm so sorry about this." He wiped his brow with his shirtsleeve. "We think it started in the back. I can take you around. That loaner cop, Lance, is back there already. Said something about calling in an arson specialist."

"Do *you* think it's arson?" Ryder asked as they tramped over the grass that had been ground into sooty mud between the fire crew and all the water.

"Difficult to say for sure. But I think he may have a point since the fire seems to have moved so fast."

"How soon can I go in? See what might be salvaged?" There might be something she could recover.

"After the investigation. If it's stable enough to enter," McCready answered.

Ryder grunted. "Who called it in?"

"Actually, I did." Frank shoved his hands in the pockets of his jumpsuit. "I was driving to my place."

Mike narrowed her eyes at the man's back. He'd left the Pink Petals before she'd gone on stage. And if he went with, or more likely followed, Val, she was staying at trailers near the marina, north of town. And the chief's home was over on the far eastern side of the lake abutting the national forest. How could he have seen the flames from the road, unless they'd already been high enough before he made the turn?

Weenie and Officer Kessler stood together at the rear of the shotgun house that had been her home, contained all her things, including the only pictures she had of her brother from his time in the service, their childhood.

"Hey, Chief." Kessler waved at Frank and met him halfway. "Did you see these broken windows?"

"Not that unusual."

Maybe not at Frank's house, but it was damn unusual for Mike's home.

"Two of them, the glass is on the inside, and the rest blew outward." Kessler's tone was smug.

Was that significant?

"My guys likely busted those two to get access."

Kessler paused. "I've put calls into the State and the Feds. But we need to get moving on this. The convention attendees are going to be returning home if they haven't started leaving already. That'll make it harder to question folks if we identify any witnesses."

"You instructed Val to stay in town?" Ryder asked.

Val had been nasty about Mike's article earlier. Nasty enough to burn down the *Peat*?

"Yep," the officer confirmed. "And Tony's two dance buddies. They weren't happy. Got jobs they need to get back to."

The details piled up as the people around her dissected what could have happened. She catalogued it all, like a trained reporter. But the longer she stared at the place she'd called home, the less able she was to move. It was impossible to tell what color the building had been from the back because the fire had been concentrated on the part of the house she lived in, not the offices.

Her boss sauntered over.

"Edwina." Thankfully Ryder could speak.

"Ryder." The council chair was perfectly made up as if she were going to a meeting instead of being awoken in the middle of the night to an emergency.

"I assume all of this is insured," Ryder said.

"Well, of course—the structure and the contents related to *The Daily Peat* are. You'd have to ask Mikaela about her renter's insurance."

Renter's insurance. The two words stabbed into Mike's gut. She'd been meaning to get that, but it was expensive, and she'd been busy reviving the online paper, and then with Heather's wedding... At least her bridesmaid dress was still at the tailor's with Heather's wedding gown. They'd decided to do the final fitting together when Heather got to Daisy on Monday. Technically, it was already Sunday.

"I don't know if it will be enough," Weenie said, bringing Mike back from the wedding angst.

"Enough for what?" Mike asked, her voice croaky.

"To rebuild. We may have to move *The Peat* into the community center offices, and we will, at least for the short term."

The idea of seeing that woman every day made an already

terrible situation worse. Having the only newspaper office with the town officials would make reporting any real news difficult. Mike dreaded the idea of having Weenie and the other council members looking over her shoulder and possibly trying to influence her reporting.

Headline: Peat's Posts Buried by Busybody Pols

"She has her work laptop with her," Ryder said. "It wasn't inside. Aside from a printer, which I have, and internet, which I also have, what does she need the office for?"

"Well, Ryder, honey, the council isn't going to pay to host *The Daily Peat* at your place, even if she is your girlfriend." Weenie's hands went to her hips, and she cocked one up.

Mike swallowed down her disgust that the woman could be jovial in the midst of Mike's nightmare.

No way she could deal with working out of the Community Center long term. Depending on the council's decision regarding the rebuild, it might be time to look for a new job, which would mean leaving Daisy. She glanced at Ryder. That conversation could wait.

Ryder slung his arm around Mike's shoulders. "There's nothing else we can do here. Let's get some sleep."

"Just a quick nap. We have church in a few hours."

Ryder closed his eyes. "Right."

"You don't have to go. But I need to be there to finish my article on the Cowbells and Crops. I may not have an office, but, like you said, the internet didn't burn down." And if she *was* leaving, it wasn't going to be on a bad note. She'd finish the job she started.

Ryder led the way back to the truck, and they returned to his place without another word. He pulled into the big garage bay and turned the truck off. "You know you can stay with me as long as you want. Forever, even."

She leaned across the bench seat and kissed him. "Thank

you." She held back all the words that could have followed starting with "but." Instead, she said, "Let's get some rest."

RYDER MADE sure Mike was asleep before he snuck out of the bedroom to send an email to his buddy with fed connections in the Houston office. If his guy could tell him who they were sending to investigate the arson, he'd be able to do some advanced prep work and possibly even get the details before they went into a report. And if they sent an asshole, he'd find a way to push the state people to handle it and convince the feds it wasn't worth their time. The response depended on how seriously they weighed the fact that it was a newspaper office that had burned.

Mike may not realize how close she'd come to death, but Ryder did. And he didn't like it one bit. The fact that the fire chief had been the one to call it in and he'd been having an affair with Tony's wife didn't sit well with him either. Also, he'd like someone to answer for why the fire alarms hadn't triggered in a public building that supposedly had been inspected that summer prior to Mike moving in.

The attack on *The Daily Peat*—on Mike—only complicated an already hazy situation. Tony was dead, and he'd been an asshole in life, from everything Ryder had gathered, but who had a motive to kill the guy? Lots of people were assholes. Hell, *most* people were assholes. And still alive and kicking. What made Tony different?

Ryder sent the email and then texted Ike, hoping he hadn't left with his boat, asking if he would be willing to meet for lunch after church. Another set of eyes, ones that hadn't had their girlfriend's house burned down, could be useful.

Soft snores emerged from the bedroom. One last thing

before he rejoined her. He logged into the web host for the security cameras and reviewed the footage from the time they left *The Peat* with Mike's things, to the time the fire trucks arrived. Nothing at the front. East side, zilch. On the west side, a dark shadow passed through the frame. Not enough to even guess if it was a man or a woman. Ryder noted the timestamp, 3:23 A.M. The back camera died a few moments after that. None of the intrusion sensors fired. Likely already damaged by the flames before the front door came down or the windows were broken.

After stripping off his pajama pants, Ryder slid between the sheets and spooned himself around Mike. She stirred but settled perfectly into his embrace. She fit. Why did she have to be so damn stubborn about staying with him? Although, having circumstances force her hand would only make her balk harder. He'd be lucky if she didn't start looking for a new job in the morning. If she left Daisy, he wasn't sure what he would do. Hopefully it wouldn't come to that, because he was fairly certain he'd try to chase her down and drag her back to her senses, caveman-style.

That would be a disaster.

His eyes were closed, but Ryder hadn't slept at all when the alarm on Mike's phone rang out.

She rolled out of his grasp and turned it off. "Ready for church?"

Hell no. "Absolutely."

CHAPTER THIRTEEN

MIKE, EXHAUSTED FROM THE NIGHT BEFORE AND HEARTBROKEN over the loss of her home, held Ryder's hand as he led her to a pew in the back of the nondenominational church for the final event of Cowbells and Crops. Despite the devastation to her world, she was determined to get through this final event and graciously represent the paper and the town.

According to Janelle, the church used to be Episcopalian. The building retained some of the more traditional trappings, like wood benches, stained glass, and red carpet over the sanctuary, or whatever they called the raised area in this congregation. Over the years, Mike had gone to various services, and she'd figured out they mainly varied by communion, choirs, and candles. Luckily, the people in charge, no matter what title they went by, always announced what the attendees were expected to do. And since she wasn't baptized anywhere, as far as she knew, she never took communion.

"Have you been here before?" Mike asked Ryder as he flipped through the Bible.

"Not in years."

People meandered down the main aisle, searching for

friends or the best place to sit based on some unknown equation that weighted the various locations.

When Weenie showed up, Mike had to clench her teeth to keep her jaw from falling open. She was almost certain the woman was a member of the Baptist church, but maybe she was putting on a show for the lingering conference attendees. Val and Frank were seated toward the front but with a good amount of space between their shoulders. Lance Kessler sauntered in wearing his khaki police uniform and took the pew across the aisle from Mike. He gave a friendly nod in their direction, the light from the windows glinting off his blond head, but Ryder didn't respond, too engrossed in whatever New Testament story he was reading toward the back of the Bible.

Olive passed by, taking a seat diagonally behind Weenie. It still blew Mike's mind that the owner of the strip club and the chair of the town council were related. Although, they had more in common than Weenie would probably admit, at least with their dominatrix ways. Olive whispered to a couple seated in the same row—Chuck and Berta Ann. Berta Ann wasn't in uniform, so Lance must technically be on duty.

The pastor, who would be marrying Heather and Jason, entered the stage at the same moment Tank dropped into the last pew behind Lance Kessler. Was he there to keep tabs on his ex-wife? Tank always worked Sunday mornings, either providing breakfast for the Bloom guests or prepping for brunch he served later in the day. At least he always had for the last few months.

A greeting rang out through the room, echoing off the walls. Mike turned her attention to Pastor Hill and made the required response. A small choir sat to one side, but there were no lit candles that she could see. Mike settled in but spent more time watching the crowd, who seemed completely mundane, stripped of their leather, leashes, and fur suits. The choir was good, small but in tune and upbeat.

When it came time for the sermon, Mike tensed. That moment was the point when things could get dicey. Pastors came in two varieties: really good and complete torture. Some faked you out by starting off well but then going long beyond what was a reasonable amount of time for a lecture. Some bombed from the get-go—too aggressive and condescending, or boring to the point of crying. Pastor Hill had potential.

He read a couple of scriptures and then expounded. As he continued, Mike focused on his words.

"Being made in the image of God means it behooves you to be true to yourself, to act as God made you. Are you being faithful to the mission and the vision God has for your life?"

Good question. Had she strayed off her path? She'd come to Daisy accidentally, chasing a lead on her brother's death. But after getting mixed up in a murder, she'd been lulled into complacency. A good job, a great—if somewhat bossy—boyfriend, and a sweet small town had distracted her from finding her brother's killer.

Why *had* she agreed to remain in Daisy?

Ryder said he could help her and that he was digging into some things. Based on the conversation she'd eavesdropped on, he was true to his word, but what had she really learned about what happened to David?

Nothing.

And what the hell did Ryder do for a living? He had a mechanic shop, and he did repairs for the people in town, but it wasn't a booming business. She glanced over at him. He had put the Bible back in the rack and was stretched out, hands resting on his abs, seeming to listen to the sermon and nodding occasionally.

She glanced across the aisle. Lance was stiff backed, and instead of focusing on the pastor, his gaze washed over everyone else. He caught Mike's eye and smirked. Odd. Maybe she'd misread his reaction or he was judging her for not paying attention. She turned back to face the correct direction for the remainder of the service. The pastor put himself squarely in the good category when he finished up quickly. The choir sang another song, and then they were released with a blessing of peace and a wish of safe travels until they could all be together again next year.

After shaking the pastor's hand on the way out, Ryder tugged Mike to the side. "I have to call Ike. We're supposed to meet for lunch."

Ryder wandered off, phone in hand. Mike lingered alone in the grassy church yard under a cloudless blue sky. Most of the crowd bee-lined for trucks attached to RVs or sedans with out-of-state plates. The convention was over—and it had provided a convenient cover for killing—but a criminal still had to be found.

The two men who had been backstage at the dance with Tony followed Val, and they all stopped out of earshot. Based on the hand movements and facial expressions, it seemed like a tense conversation. Officer Kessler took a couple of steps in her direction but then glanced around. After meeting Mike's eye, he turned in the opposite direction and strode away. Chief McCready hovered a couple of yards from Val, arms crossed. Mike took out her phone and sent Heather a quick text to call when she had time.

"Mike." Olive crossed into her line of sight. The strip-club owner, dressed in a summer-weight pastel blue wraparound dress, blended perfectly with the crowd.

Mike toed her canvas shoe into the dirt and smoothed her black t-shirt. "Good morning, Olive."

"Are you doing okay after last night? Didn't see much of you after you left the stage." The Pink Petals *performance* seemed like a million years ago.

"Sorry about that." Mike had left without saying goodbye. "Ryder rushed me out of there so fast."

114

She chuckled. "I bet he did." Olive patted Mike's arm. "You were great. Much better than your pole-dancing."

Mike winced at the reminder of her one-and-only attempt at stripping last summer.

Weenie, dressed in a wintergreen sheath with matching heels, marched down the stairs toward them. "Mike. Are you okay?"

"As good as I can be."

"That's right. *The Peat.*" Olive put her hand to her chest. "I'm so sorry."

Not as sorry as Mike was, but she appreciated the kind words.

"I got the call as I was leaving your place," Weenie told Olive.

"That was late."

"Apparently Frank saw smoke after he left Val. He called Lance, and Lance called me since Daisy owns the building."

"What happened?" Olive sounded more concerned than gossipy.

"We don't know yet. Lance is getting a specialist to come out. He put a call into the Houston federal office right away." Weenie glanced around. "In fact, I should find out if there's an update."

"He already left." Mike pointed in the direction he'd gone.

"Lance was here?" Weenie asked. "Never mind. I'll catch him at the station."

As soon as Weenie was out of earshot, Mike asked Olive, "Why was Weenie with you so late? I thought you two barely talked?"

Olive barked out a laugh and quickly covered her mouth with her fingertips. "She was trying to butter me up. Wants me to be the coordinator for the Cowbells conference next year. She's worried Val will move it if we don't start the publicity soon. With all the money it brings into Daisy, Weenie's worried about the loss."

"Isn't it Val's conference?"

"Not really. The town has trademarked the name and pays to host the website. But she could change the name, and if they don't have anyone to run it—"

"Why would Val move it? I thought she and Weenie were friends." Mike asked.

"From what I know, Tony was the one who was adamant about it staying in Daisy, even though it's kind of outgrown us. Weenie and I chatted with two of the committee members at the Petals, Albert and Kenny. They said lot of the participants had trouble finding places to stay within a reasonable distance. Even the RV slots in the park were full."

"Are you going to take over?"

Olive gave her a Mona Lisa smile. "Maybe."

Clearly the negotiations hadn't finished the night before. What was Olive holding out for?

Olive said her goodbyes when Ryder rejoined Mike.

"Come on." Ryder tugged her hand. "Giang's going to open Transplanted T'weeds for us."

She followed him toward the truck. "What? Why?"

"Because aside from the few things at my place, until you wash what you're wearing, your clothing choices are limited to the dress you wore last night and your bridesmaid dress. You need more clothes."

"Fine." As much as she adored the secondhand clothing store, she sighed at the prospect of shopping. "I thought you had to meet Ike?" And hopefully get more information on her brother's non-suicide—the whole reason she'd ended up in Daisy in the first place.

"Lacy has to get home. Her company's being targeted for a hostile takeover." Lacy was a CEO? No wonder their boat was so nice.

Mike's stomach growled. "Can we visit Phō King first?"

"Of course." Ryder grinned, and damn he was beautiful.

"I don't know who likes that name more, you or Giang," Mike teased as she followed Ryder to his truck.

At the restaurant, they sat at one of the few empty tables across from the hand-painted koi garden mural that filled the opposite wall. Tan, Giang's sister, brought out their bowls almost as soon as they sat down.

"Guess we've gotten in a rut," Mike said as she scraped the bean sprouts and herbs into the hot broth.

Ryder grunted. "Not a bad thing."

Mike wasn't so sure. She'd only lived in Daisy for a few months, and already she was so entrenched in routine. Was that really how her life should be in her twenties? But then, Heather was about to get married. It wasn't like they went on many adventures before that, but there had been the possibility. They *could* have done wild things or traveled or become different people. After this weekend, those options were dwindling. And if Mike moved in with Ryder, wouldn't that be almost the same thing? Falling into routines was a lot like falling into dependency. Easy to do and hard to recover from when it's ripped away.

After lunch, Mike dug into the circular racks of Transplanted T'weeds that filled what had likely been an old five and dime back in the day. She found two pairs of jeans, three funny tees, and a decent sweater. The shoes were a bust, mostly heels, but her high-tops would work fine with jeans. It wasn't like she dressed up for work before the fire.

"You sure you don't need anything else?" Ryder asked as they waited in front of the glass cabinet filled with fake jewelry while Giang finished calculating the total.

"I can wait until I have time to go Houston. I'm just going to be running around doing wedding stuff or writing." Plus, she couldn't afford much more. Not when she'd need to find a place to live, either in Daisy or Houston. But that was a problem for after the wedding. One emergency at a time.

Ryder tucked her bag, a paper grocery sack stamped with a big red flower, behind the seat of the truck while Mike climbed in on the passenger side. Her phone rang. "It's Heather. Mind if I take it?"

He shook his head.

"Hey, Heather. You got my text?"

Silence dragged on a second too long. "What's wrong?"

"Nothing," Mike said, avoiding the list of things Heather could worry about. "I was just wondering, did I leave any stuff at the apartment? Since you're coming here tomorrow, I figured I should ask. Get the rest of my stuff cleared out."

"Maybe? I think a coat and some boots? I can check. But why? I know you. Something's happened—I can hear it in your voice, and I had a horrible dream last night that everything was ruined."

"Nothing's ruined exactly, but there was a fire." She'd lost everything, most likely. But not people. Not anyone she loved, and the rest was stuff and mementos.

"Oh no. At the Bloom? Please tell me the inn did *not* catch on fire."

"Nope. Not the Bloom." Mike took a calming breath. "*The Peat* burned down last night."

"Oh my god. Are you okay?"

"I was at Ryder's, but pretty much everything else is gone. Not sure exactly what I might be able to salvage. I have to wait until the investigators are done before I can maybe go in to get whatever's left."

"Honey. I'm so sorry."

"It's fine. I'm fine. I just figured if there was anything at your place, I could use it."

"Of course. I'll be there around seven. Can I see you when I get in?"

Mike agreed, looking forward to spending time with Heather but dreading having to fill her in on the other stuff that was happening. Ryder pulled into his garage and got her bag. She hung up with Heather as the garage door lowered, took the bag from him, and went to the utility room tucked under the stairs that led to his apartment. "I'm going to start some laundry and do some writing. Do you need anything washed?"

"I'm good. Gonna make some calls. You want to use my office?"

"Perfect." Not really. Her little home at the back of *The Daily Peat*, the first space of her very own, had been perfect.

She started the washer with her new-used clothes, and Ryder brought her computer downstairs. "Here you go, M."

And he was perfect. As a boyfriend, she couldn't ask for more. She gave him a lingering kiss in the doorway, an apology for being grumpy and appreciation for him seeing to everything she needed. "Thank you."

"No problem."

She meant it for more than the computer delivery, and lunch, and finding her clothes. He was an amazing person, and she should be happy that she had a place to stay for as long as she wanted. But living at the garage was like wearing a sweater when the arms were too narrow. Constricting. Claustrophobic. No matter how much she might like it, nothing she could do would make it fit.

She opened her laptop and tried to formulate pithy sentences about the Cowbells and Crops conference. If she didn't work and create positive content about the community, what reason would the council have to restore her home? And if she didn't live in Daisy, where would she go?

119

CHAPTER FOURTEEN

M IKE'S PHONE RANG, AND SHE GLANCED AT THE SCREEN. FINALLY. Ryder, seated across from her at his small table, didn't seem to notice, just kept eating. Mike wiped her hands on a napkin and dropped it on her dinner plate then tapped the green circle.

"I'm here," Heather's voice pealed through the speaker.

Mike squealed with her. "This is really happening. You're getting married."

"I'm at the inn. Can you come over?"

"Are you sure you're not too tired from the drive?" Mike asked.

Ryder cleared her dishes from the table.

"No way. I'm totally amped up on caffeine, and I have a bottle of wine with our name on it. And I ordered an appetizer plate from Bay Leaves."

"Yum. Anything from there is delicious." Mike glanced up at Ryder, who was washing away the leavings of their barbecue dinner. He dried his hands and pulled his keys off the hook, raising an eyebrow at her.

"I'm on my way." She ended the call. "You sure you don't mind taking me?"

"Not at all. You'll be drinking."

"I'll probably stay the night." Mike studied his face, but he didn't so much as twitch.

He grunted an acknowledgement, and Mike threw some freshly washed clothes in her bag before they were on their way. After a short, silent drive, they pulled up in front of Bloom with a View. Mike leaned across the bench of the truck and gave Ryder a peck on the cheek. "Thank you."

"Text me if you need a ride tomorrow."

His offer made the area between her shoulder blades itch. She shouldn't be avoiding him, but the fire had forced her to move in with him before she was ready. Heather's room at the inn offered a reprieve, and Mike wasn't about to miss the opportunity. But none of this was his fault. She gave Ryder a real kiss, and desire shot down to her toes. Damn, the man could kiss. Before she could beg him to come get her in a couple of hours, she retreated, bursting out of the truck and jogging up the path to the inn.

She knocked on Heather's door, and her best friend opened it a second later. They'd barely closed the door before they were hugging and jumping up and down.

"I can't believe this is finally happening," Heather said after they calmed down. She twisted off the cap of the bottle of white wine and poured two plastic cups full.

"Cheers." Mike held out her glass to Heather. "To my bestie who thinks four months is a forever-long engagement."

Heather laughed and then took a sip of wine. "I have a couple things for you."

"Wait. I have something for you, too. Since this is like your bachelorette party." Mike dug into her laptop case to retrieve the perfectly wrapped rectangular box that thankfully had been spared from the fire since it was in with the dress Ryder had bought for the night at the Petals.

Heather carefully undid the wrapping paper on one end and

slid the box out and open. She burst out laughing. "You bought me a cock?"

"A hand-carved wood one. It's a work of art. For those nights when Jason's traveling or whatever. I mean, always hard, guaranteed."

"It's beautiful. Thank you." Heather hugged her and then placed the rosewood cock back in its box. She tucked it into one of her suitcases and pulled out two pairs of jeans that Mike had left behind, along with a scarf, a pair of old boots, and some blue flats. That's where those had been.

Heather's face dropped into a serious line. "Now what the hell is going on here? How did your office burn down?"

Mike sorted out where to begin while Heather zipped up the case and moved it off the bed. Better to rip off the bandage. "There was another murder."

Heather whipped around. "Another one? What the hell is with this place?"

"I think it's just kind of random. It doesn't seem related to what happened this summer or to my brother."

"I don't know if that's better or worse. Who died this time?"

"A guy named Tony." Mike sat on the bed. It would take a while to explain. "He and his wife were here for the Cowbells and Crops conference. In fact, they coordinated it."

Heather set her half-empty cup on the nightstand. "How'd he die? Who found him?"

Tony's dead face flashed in front of Mike's eyes. She sipped her wine. "I did."

"Oh my god." Heather crossed her arms.

"When I was measuring for your tent."

"He died here?" Heather scanned the room. "At the Bloom?"

"Not exactly. More like in the woods just past the yard."

"That is so fucking creepy." Heather brushed her hands over her arms and then peered out the window, which made no

HELL HATH NO FURRY

sense since her room faced the marina. "Did they find who did it?"

"Not yet."

"I bet it was the wife. It's always the spouse in the movies."

"Maybe." Mike was glad Heather wasn't more upset. She'd been dying to talk through what she'd found out and try to make sense of it all. "But it would have had to be someone really strong. Tony's face was bashed in with a leather dildo."

Heather turned from the window. "Did you say…dildo?"

Mike snorted. "Yeah. A sand-filled leather dildo."

Heather covered her laugh with her hand. "His poor wife. Can you imagine the gossip? But yeah, it would have to be someone really strong. Where did they get the dildo? And did you know when you say dildo five times, it starts to sound pretty funny."

"Sounds weird the first time. Who came up with that word for a fake cock?" Mike shook her head. English was so bizarre. "There were vendors selling all kinds of sex toys at the convention. That's where I found yours—hand-carved, one-of-a-kind." Mike sipped her wine.

"But they have ones like the one used on Tony?"

Mike nodded. "That vendor's been at previous cons, too. There was also a dildo at the demo that night, the spanking one?"

"A dildo? For spanking?"

Heather burst out laughing at the same time as Mike.

Heather straightened up first. "The demo you went to? Was it that dildo?"

"Not sure." Mike made a plan to follow-up with Chuck to confirm if she still had her toy. "Chuck and Berta Ann did the class, but I don't know if theirs is missing."

"*Deputy* Berta Ann?"

"Yeah, totally bared her ass in front of everyone and—" Mike snapped her mouth closed. She wasn't ready to discuss that she'd been spanked in public during the conference.

"Could Chuck have done it?"

"There's no reason she would want him dead. I mean, she escorted him out at the end because he was being an ass, but she wasn't super angry or anything."

"Who else was there?"

"Tank."

Heather's eyes went wide. "The chef? What does he have to do with anything?"

"He's the wife's ex-husband."

Heather's jaw dropped. "Whoa."

"In fact, Val accused him of doing it." And he had tried to stop Mike from walking the grounds that day.

"Tank is a teddy bear. Was there bad blood?"

"I don't think Tank liked Tony, but mainly he didn't think the guy was good enough for Val. But like you said, Tank's so nice. It would have to be something horrible—"

"Was Tony beating Val?"

"Might have been the other way around." Mike leaned closer to Heather. "Val's a Domme. And Tony was a furry."

"A furry?"

"The conference was a combo for BDSM and furries. He had a tiger costume. Which he was wearing at the time he died. Except for the head obviously. But whoever killed him put the head over his face."

"Gross. Someone must have hated him bad."

Mike considered the statement. "Hated's a strong word."

"Murder's kind of a big deal."

"His furry friends were mad at him for ditching them for the dance competition. And Frank McCready, our fire chief, is having an affair with Val." Mike should have asked Ryder if anyone had interviewed the dance crew.

"The Daisy fire chief is having an affair with the dead guy's wife?"

Mike shrugged one shoulder. The more she explained, the crazier everything sounded. Like a badly scripted reality show. "Well, they had an open marriage, I guess."

"Did Val tell you that? She could be lying."

"Good point." Mike held up her glass for a refill. "But Tony got around, too. He and Letty—"

"The naughty baker?" Heather hooted. "The hot-pants-wearing cougar doing the food for my rehearsal party?"

"Yeah. Her. I heard they hooked up, so I think the open marriage thing is true."

Heather refilled their glasses. "This kind of stuff happens all the time on those *Housewives* shows, but they don't kill each other...mostly."

Mike shrugged. "Whoever the killer is probably set my office on fire."

"Wait. What?" Heather set her wine down. "You said your office caught on fire, not that someone set it on fire."

Mike paced over to the window. "I think they might have been trying to kill me."

"Oh my god. Why?"

"I don't really know. I've been asking questions. Mainly for my articles about the event, not about the murder. Val was worried that I might write an article that would make the big papers. I can't imagine they'd be interested in anything I wrote. Ryder has been helping out on the investigation because, you know, Berta Ann was kind of implicated at first as maybe being involved. And Donny is out of town, so there's a loaner officer from the county. He doesn't know everyone as well as Ryder." Mike held out her empty hand. "So..."

"This feels bigger than a love triangle."

"Maybe. I don't know what else it could be."

"Are you sure it doesn't have something to do with what Karla was into before she turned up dead?"

"Nothing connects to that. At least not that I've found."

Heather held up the half-empty bottle of wine. "More?"

"We have your final fitting in the morning."

"Better to have a little room. I plan on eating and drinking at the reception."

"Good call." Mike held out her glass again. Heather's words sat heavy in her gut. Did the murder have something to do with her brother, David? Was that why she'd been targeted, too?

RYDER HATED SLEEPING ALONE. He'd asked Janelle to call if Mike or Heather left the inn, so Mike had stayed with Heather. And technically, Mike still hadn't agreed to live with him, even though she had nowhere else to go. Not that he was comfortable with being a last resort. If only she wanted to be with him as much as he wanted her to move in. There had to be something he could do to shift her thinking, convince her she should move in. No time to solve that problem. He had an appointment with Lance to help interview Kenny and Albert, Tony's dance partners.

Before he went to the station, he stopped at The Flour Bed to pick up donuts. It had been a while since he'd brought treats, and maybe a little sweetness and a casual vibe would get the guys talking more than a formal process. Lance might have a different plan, but Ryder had no problem running roughshod over the man, especially since Mike had been threatened. And Ryder's intuition and military training left no doubt in his mind that the fire was tied to the murder.

"Got your fav," Ryder told Berta Ann as he carried the box into the station. "Strawberry ice." Ryder held back a chuckle. Mike swore everything Letty made was dirty and that the strawberry slice on the pink frosted donut looked like a tongue teasing the hole. Once she'd pointed it out, he couldn't unsee it, but the donuts were delicious and The Flour Bed was the only bakery in town.

"Thanks, Ryder." Berta Ann lifted a pastry from the box. "What brings you here?"

"Doing an interview with Lance."

"Oh, he's already back there with the guys."

Both of them together? Ryder rolled his eyes along with Berta Ann, grabbed the box, and went back to the conference room. Hopefully the situation could be fixed. Ryder rapped on the door with his knuckles then opened it without waiting.

Lance bolted up from his chair. "Ryder. Wasn't sure you were coming."

"Brought donuts. Hungry?" He set the box in the middle of the table. Donny had moved the coffee setup out of the break room before he left to make things easier for Berta Ann. Ryder had doubted the plan at the time but had to thank his cousin for the perfect opportunity to split up the party. "I'm gonna grab coffee. Anyone else?"

The two guys, both middle-aged, one balding and one with a Dunlap belly, nodded.

Lance held up his insulated cup. "I'm good."

Ryder pointed at the guy on the left. "Come with me. I could use an extra hand."

As soon as they were in the hallway with the door shut, Ryder held out his hand. "Ryder Ruiz."

"Albert Gaudraux."

"Did you have a good time at the conference? Oh, damn, sorry. Bad question." Ryder led him past the two holding cells, into the bullpen where Berta Ann was licking pink frosting off her fingers.

"Naw, that's okay. It was good overall, except for Tony obviously. I have a lot of folks I don't see except once a year at this thing."

Ryder pulled three mugs out of the shallow laminate cabinet above the coffeemaker, including Donny's favorite. It had an image of handcuffs and "I like big busts and I cannot lie." He poured out the remainder of the pot in the sink in the restroom to brew a fresh one.

Albert fidgeted with the cuticle on his thumb, looking younger. And familiar.

"You've been coming to Daisy for a while, then?"

"Yeah, I've attended the conference almost since the first."

Was it possible? "I think I remember you. Yellow C5 Corvette?"

Albert blinked at Ryder, staring hard. "You're the mechanic. Fixed the exhaust butterfly valve that stuck open. God, I miss that car." He rubbed his belly. "I think I outgrew it. Wanted something easier to get in and out of and little cheaper on the maintenance side."

"Not unusual to outgrow those hotrods. Used to have one myself. You know, you were lucky to catch me in town that year. Normally, I skip out during the convention." Avoiding the crowds and the memories.

"Damn lucky. Never did have to mess with that exhaust again. Everything else, though…"

"How did you get involved with the convention, if you don't mind me asking." Ryder dropped a little aw-shucks into his tone of voice and leaned against the counter as the first drops of fresh brew hit the carafe.

"Tony and me used to work together on the oil rigs before he moved into sales and I quit to manage construction projects. Along with Kenny, he's in sales too, we organize the furry part of the conference. But the past few years, Tony's become kind of a tyrant about it. We kept trying to talk him into moving it or even splitting it up into two events because folks do love Daisy.

Tony wouldn't budge. Of course, what did he care if the rooms were nonexistent and expensive, Val and him had the hook-up staying in Edwina's trailer by the marina for free."

"Huh?" Ryder leaned back against the counter. "Where are you and Kenny staying?"

"At the inn. We book for next year before we leave. The new dates are always set by the conference committee on the last day."

"And it's just the four of you on the committee?"

"Oh, no. Edwina Alman is on it. Has been for years now. There have been other members that come and go. We've got two right now, but I don't know if they'll stay after this. And I think Tony ditching us during the dance competition was the last straw for Kenny."

"Where did you work with Tony?"

Albert mentioned the name of a well-known oil and gas company. "Got to be too much."

"I can relate to that." Ryder poured the coffee. "Berta Ann, you need a refill?"

She hovered her hand over her mug. "I'm good."

"Hey, Albert. Would you mind keeping Berta Ann company while I go take this coffee to Kenny?"

The short man with the middle-aged tire around his middle sat at the chair in front of Berta Ann's desk. "Yeah, of course."

"One thing. Anyone you can think of who'd want to kill Tony?"

"Well." He rubbed the back of his neck. "I don't know any names or details or anything, but he was getting a lot of calls from somebody. Seemed like he was getting pressure about delivering on a promise, but I don't know what he promised to do. Had to be something around Daisy though."

"Why do you say that?"

"Just little comments. 'I'm here. No, I'll handle it. I've already been out to the new site. I told you I'd take care of it.' That kind of thing. We even came in a couple days early. And he wasn't hanging out with us, even missed our usual boy's night kickoff."

Ryder grunted. If Tony's buddy thought he was up to something, he likely was. But what? Had the crime scene team found Tony's phone or put in a request for a warrant to get the local usage details? Before he could make it back to the interview, Kenny and Lance were coming toward him in the hallway.

"I appreciate y'all coming in." Lance shook Kenny's hand at the door to the lobby. "If I have any more questions, I'll give you a call."

Albert rose and left with his buddy.

Ryder scowled at the idiot lawman, ditching the untouched mug of coffee next to the pot. He waited until the men were gone then turned on Lance. "Get anything useful?"

"They have alibis for the murder and the fire." He glanced at Ryder. "Of course, I'll verify them. I have all their contact info, but I don't think they're good for it."

Lance didn't seem to think at all. Ryder crossed his arms.

"I'm going to write this up." Lance held up a pad with a few lines of his special shorthand notes. Shouldn't take him long.

Ryder turned to the smart person in the room. "Berta Ann, I've got to take care of something, but you want to grab lunch after?"

"Sure thing." Berta Ann waved as he left.

Ryder spotted the car of the person he was looking for in the parking lot across the street. He crossed the road and entered the community center, heading to the hallway that held a few utilitarian offices for the town council. A young woman he hadn't met sat at a reception desk that looked like World War II salvage. Before he could introduce himself, Weenie appeared in the farthest office doorway.

"What brings you here?" Weenie Alman was all smiles in a pastel pink skirt suit.

"Got a minute? Need to ask you some questions about this conference."

"Of course." Weenie glared over his shoulder. "Naomi. Hold my calls."

"Yes, ma'am."

Ryder resisted rolling his eyes. "Been busy?"

"You have no idea. With the conference and trying to clean up all the messes my husband left. If I'd have known how terrible he was at running a business…" She shut the office door with a bang, the small glass pane insert rattling in its frame. "Well, that's in the past. And the council hired Naomi so we have someone manning the phones and to help me with all of this." She waved her pointy manicure around the room.

A four-drawer metal file cabinet, another dated desk with tidy piles of paper. The only nod to modernity was the black ergonomic chair. Ryder settled into a chair on his side of the desk. The padding had been pancaked decades ago. "Conference going to be here next year?"

"Why wouldn't it be?" Weenie sat in her plush rolling chair.

"Heard it might be outgrowing our little town." Ryder faked a smile.

"That's ridiculous. We have tons of rooms and rentals. Besides, we're the most accepting and inclusive town in the area. Close to two metropolitan areas and right across the border from Louisiana. Only those two fool friends of Tony want to move it. Probably because they've screwed their way through everyone who would give them the time of day. Hoping for a new crowd if they find a new venue. Cowbells and Crops is a Daisy event. If they move it, they start from scratch, including a new name. They can't have my logo, so good luck."

"Guess you knew Tony well."

"I'm closer with Valerie."

Made sense. Although two Dommes could get into some serious power struggles.

"How's she handling this?"

"Well, of course she's just devastated."

Ryder admired Weenie's shift to Southern belle.

"I *insisted* she come stay with me at the house. When it was the two of them, the trailer made sense, and it's so much closer to most of the activities. But she needs time to mourn. I'm so glad I could be there for her in her time of need."

Ryder waited for Weenie to pull out a handkerchief and dab nonexistent tears from her eyes, but apparently, she wasn't going to take the performance that far. "You were at the spanking demo with them?"

"I try to attend as many of the sessions and competitions as I can." She patted her bleached-blonde updo. "I'm the face of Daisy now."

Ryder wasn't going to touch that one. "I heard Tony had to be escorted out."

Weenie huffed. "The man had no subtlety. Hitting on everyone within arm's reach."

"What did Valerie think about that?"

"They had an open marriage. She kept herself occupied."

"Did you notice anyone follow Tony out? Anyone overly interested in the spanking tool?"

"No."

Interesting. She never answered with one word. "What about after the demo? Did Valerie go back to the trailer?"

"She had the dance competition. After that, we went to Olive's bar for a drink. We were meeting people there."

"The Pink Petals?"

She pursed her painted lips that perfectly matched her suit. "Such a tacky name. But yes. We stayed a couple of hours."

"Who'd you meet?

Weenie narrowed her eyes. "Am I being interrogated, Ryder?"

"Not at all. There's just a whole lot of folks around, and you being the face of Daisy and the primary event liaison, I knew you'd know more than anyone else about what happened that night." He gave her his best sympathy-inducing look. "I just hoped you could help."

"Ryder, you know I'll help in any way I can. We met some of the other committee members, Albert and Kenny and the two women who volunteered this year. Although, I don't know why they bothered. They haven't lifted a hand to do anything. Valerie and I have worked our fingers to the bone. And the thanks we get is the men pushing to move it."

"Valerie stay with you that night?"

"No. Frank picked her up. Anything else?" Weenie pushed back from her desk and stood.

Val had lied about where she'd been. Ryder stood. "Thanks, Weenie."

"I hope Officer Kepler finds out who did this."

"Kessler."

"Whatever."

Ryder paused at the reception desk and introduced himself to Naomi Evans. She'd just started the job that morning. Moved to town from a ranch not too far away. He left his card with her and made a note to introduce her to Mike. Naomi would need a friend, working for Weenie.

He called Berta Ann and asked her to meet him at Jerry's. If he had to see Kessler again so soon, he'd lose his appetite to anger. He obviously hadn't interviewed Weenie, or she would've complained about the man questioning her. Had the county sent their most useless hack to fill in for Donny? And why had Weenie acted like she didn't know the officer's name?

On the front deck of Jerry's, Ryder waited for Berta Ann so they could order together.

She waved from the sidewalk as she approached. "Thanks for getting me out of there."

They ordered their burgers and fries from Jorge, the owner

of the Grateful Dead–inspired restaurant. Ryder held out two twenties, but Jorge waived him off as usual. Sometimes Ryder felt guilty the locals gave him stuff, but he made sure to always make it up to them with car repairs and anything else he could do to help out. Once he'd been adopted by the town, they'd never let him go. Even when he was deployed. Boxes always found their way to his location—sometimes worse for wear, but always filled with love.

Berta Ann and Ryder took a seat at one of the open picnic tables that filled the long narrow room covered with dancing bear and skull with lightning bolt motifs and memorabilia. Before their food arrived, Chuck came in, went to the counter, and then joined them.

"Hope you don't mind," Chuck said as she swung a leg over the bench and sat close to Berta Ann.

"Not at all. Saves me a trip to the bait shop," Ryder said.

"Well hell. Then I'm leaving so you'll have to buy something." She laughed at her joke.

"You see plenty of me in there." Although, he hadn't done a lot of fishing since Mike had come to town last summer. He made a note to fix that.

"How's your day going?" Chuck asked Berta Ann.

The deputy frowned. "No worse."

"Kessler giving you a hard time?"

"Not exactly. He's just not on top of things the way Donny is. I finally filed for the search warrant to get the LUDs for the vic's phone. He was supposed to do it, but he kept 'forgetting.' I swear, he's more interested in what he's going to have for lunch than finding a murderer."

Jorge delivered their baskets of burgers and fries with some friendly banter, and Ryder waited until the food was mostly gone before he asked the question that had been burning in his mind. "Are you missing your demonstration tool?"

Chuck paled and grabbed Berta Ann's hand. "We didn't realize it was gone, and we're sick about it."

"Toward the end of the demo, it got a little crazy. People were crowding, asking questions." Berta Ann's voice wobbled.

"It was overwhelming for Berty. I had to bum-rush Tony out of the building. Started getting handsy."

"I thought Chuck had packed everything up," Berta said.

"And I thought Berty had tucked away the dildo."

"Anyone else hanging around?" Ryder asked.

"Could have been anyone." Chuck glanced at Berta Ann. "Most of the town was there. Maybe all of them, if you count the ones in costume."

"You mean the furries." Which meant no one might know with certainty who had or had not been at the demo.

"Yeah. A couple of them we know, Albert and Kenny. But some I'd never seen before."

"What did you two do after the demo?" Ryder had to ask since he couldn't count on Kessler.

"Went home." Berta Ann blushed.

Chuck patted Berta Ann's hand. "We had to close out that scene." Chuck raised her eyebrows at Ryder. "I'm sure you understand."

Ryder didn't miss the reference to his scene with Mike. Theirs wasn't a great alibi but was more than likely true. Chuck might punch Tony for touching Berta Ann, but Ryder couldn't see the mild-mannered, fly-tying bait shop owner getting worked up enough over some grab-ass to kill someone. The questions remained. Who had, and why?

CHAPTER FIFTEEN

MIKE SHIFTED ON THE RED VELVET CHAIR AND FIDDLED WITH HER phone. She could call Ryder while Heather was attended to in the dressing room—really the back bedroom of the house the tailor used for her business. Heather's wedding dress was beautiful, although far more layers of fabric than Mike would ever consider wearing. The seamstress had identified a few necessary adjustments. Mike had no idea what the woman was talking about, but Heather had nodded in agreement, so the fixes must be real. Mike's phone lit with a text.

Ryder: *Where are you?*

Could he sense she'd been thinking about him?

Mike: *Wedding dress fitting.*

Ryder: *Everything okay?*

Mike: *Yep.*

Mike: *We're having lunch next and then a few more errands. I might stay the night with Heather again.*

Seeing her best friend in a poofy white-wedding dress—something she'd never thought she'd wanted—had done something weird to her heart. If she went back to the garage, she might cave in to his demand to live with him beyond the temporary emergency.

Speaking of… She dialed her boss's cellphone.

"Mikaela, how are you?" The imperious tone grated like nails on a chalkboard.

"Fine. Just checking on what's going on with the building."

Edwina let out a condescending titter. "Oh, bless your heart. I hope you aren't going to call me every two days. These things take time. I'm not sure the police report has been filed. We've yet to hear from the arson investigator. Then, of course, we'll have to submit a claim to the insurance company…"

Hadn't the woman told her to call if she needed anything? "Should I find another place to live? Another job?"

"I don't *think* so. I saw the articles you posted yesterday. You did a fine job capturing the spirit of the conference and presenting it in a very positive light. That's exactly the kind of news we like to see published about our little town. *Ryder* said you could keep working. Is your next deadline a problem?"

Ryder said? The woman treated her like a rebellious teenager. But she also provided a paycheck. Mike gritted her teeth. "No problem at all."

"Why don't you take down my secretary's number. Naomi can keep you up to date on the situation with the newspaper office."

Mike dutifully noted the number and the hint not to call Edwina about *The Peat* again, even though it had been more than an office. It had been her home.

Heather popped out from the back bedroom of the house dressed in her regular clothes. "Ready?"

"I'm starving." Mike pocketed her phone. Ryder hadn't responded to her last text.

"Where should we go? My treat." Heather checked the notifications on her own phone and smiled.

"There's a new barbecue place outside of town I heard about.

I've been meaning to try it so I can do an article. I need something for my next post."

Heather finished sending a text. "I hope it's traditional Texas and not some crazy fusion thing."

"We'll find out." It would be easier for Mike to make fusion sound interesting in her post, but her stomach agreed with Heather.

They drove down a two-lane tree-lined road, seemingly headed to the middle of nowhere. Around a bend, an unlit neon sign came into view. It was a huge red star with a bendy white arrow and the words Junk's in the Trunk in big blue letters. Mike stopped the car and leaned out the driver's window to take a picture with her phone. More pictures meant fewer words. "Unusual name for a meat shack."

They parked in the lot filled with muddy four-by-four trucks, sleek sedans, and SUVs in all the current colors.

"Popular place," Heather said as she closed the door on Mike's tiny clunker.

A six-foot wood fence surrounded the property with a gate wide enough to drive a tractor trailer through. Well beyond the fence, picnic tables were lined up under a couple of large metal awnings. A fire pit surrounded by Adirondack chairs sat dormant in a sea of pea gravel that covered every square inch of the property not paved with slab concrete. The smell of mesquite fire wafted up from the repurposed trunks of cars that filled the far corner of the corral. Interesting solution for smoking meat, and it explained the name. Mostly. Mike snapped a couple more pictures.

Groups of men in jeans sucked barbecue sauce off their fingers and sipped root beer from glass bottles. Eyes followed Mike and Heather as they made their way to the cavernous red metal building. Sliding doors had been pushed back, and the interior was crowded with more people and picnic tables covered with red-and-white-checked oilcloth. Vintage metal signs advertising colas and orange drinks dotted the walls, along with rodeo posters and the odd piece of retired ranching equipment.

The line moved quickly, and Heather and Mike grabbed drinks from an ice-filled trough as they passed. A stack of various desserts filled another metal-lined refrigerator trough. Mike grabbed a banana pudding cup and held it up to Heather, but she shook her head.

"What can I get y'all?" A big man with rolled up sleeves on his t-shirt leaned forward through the cutout window in the wood paneling that separated the food prep area from the dining room.

Mike glanced up at the chalkboard above the man's head. "Brisket lunch special with potato salad."

"Rib special with coleslaw," Heather said.

The man hollered their order over his shoulder to other equally large men wielding cleavers. He ripped off a piece of paper with his indecipherable scribbles and handed it to Mike. "Pay at the end."

Mike got to the cashier first, but Heather bumped her out of the way. "I'm buying. You've done so much for the wedding."

Rather than argue, Mike asked the cashier, "Do you have a printed menu or a to-go menu?"

The woman shook her head and totaled their order.

"A website?" Mike persisted.

"Nope. People know what we're selling or they don't. Word a mouth's all we need."

Accurate, since Mike had heard of the place from the bear furry, Kenny. As soon as Heather got her change, a cafeteria tray filled with baskets of meat and rolls and Styrofoam cups of slaw and salad appeared.

"Inside or out?" Heather asked Mike as she took the tray.

There weren't many empty spots inside, but it might be better to remain where the employees could see them rather than try their luck with the workmen who'd already paid them too much attention. Part of her missed the protection Ryder's constant presence provided.

They found space at the end of a table in the far corner in front of a group of men in suits. The quantity of people who came through the space was astounding. People must be driving for miles, because there weren't that many residents in Daisy and the surrounding area. Unless they were *all* eating barbecue on a Tuesday. Despite the cashier's denial of a menu, the majority didn't seem to place an order at all, just picked up a bag at the cashier. There must be a way to order online or by phone. Even the temporary police officer, Kessler, came through the line with Chief McCready. Maybe she'd come back with Ryder. He had a way of getting information from people.

It sucked that her first thought was to rely on him and that she needed him at all for an article that should be a no brainer. She'd have to come up with a different angle or a completely different topic for her fast-approaching deadline.

Mike licked the last of her pudding off the plastic spoon and considered licking the cup clean, too.

"Oh my god. That was so good." Heather tugged a wet towelette from its foil wrapper and wiped her fingers. "If I'd known about this place, I'd have had the rehearsal dinner here."

"I only heard about it this weekend. No website."

"Probably too far for everyone to drive anyway. And I didn't see any real beer."

"Good point." Another detail to investigate. Because she *would* find out how this place worked and write it up. Even without Ryder.

RYDER STARED AT HIS PHONE. Mike hadn't come home again. He rubbed his fist over his chest where his heart ached in a way he'd spent years avoiding. The last time, he'd tattooed a compass rose over the aching organ to remind him to listen the true direction of his heart when his mind was leading him astray. And he had been. Listening. But Mike's heart didn't seem to be in agreement.

Maybe she was thinking too much and not following her own heart, because there was no doubt that love filled the quiet spaces between them. Until she slowed down enough to recognize it, he'd have to be patient. In the meantime, he had a murderer to find and his town to protect.

Mow hopped up on the bed and began kneading Ryder's stomach with tiny kitty paws. At least someone wanted to be with him. His cat made a demanding meow. Well, loved the food he provided. Ryder rose and fed his loyal feline then started coffee. He rushed through a shower and pulled on clean black jeans. Before he had a chance to zip up, his phone rang, and he leapt to answer it.

"Ryder?" Mike's voice punched him in the gut, a note of fear in her voice.

"What's wrong?"

"They're arresting Tank."

Ryder blinked. "Who's they? Where?"

"FBI. At the inn."

"On my way." He ended the call and dropped his phone to the bed. He pulled on a t-shirt, tucked it in to his jeans. His boots were laced moments later, and he was on his motorcycle. He pulled up as the unmarked SUV pulled away with the chef. "Lance, what's going on?"

The cop swiped at his sweaty brow. "Mr. Murphy seems to be our arsonist and possibly our killer."

No fucking way. "Arsonist?"

"Guess they ran a search, and Murphy made a huge propane purchase a day before the newspaper office was torched."

Mike came running down the sidewalk toward them, her

hair askew, feet bare. He held open his arms, but she stopped before she reached him. "They took Tank."

Ryder nodded and moved his attention back to Lance.

"Seems there's a missing canister, and Mr. Murphy has no alibi for that night. Or for the night of the murder for that matter."

"The propane was for the wedding." Mike's hands were on her hips, and she glared at Lance. "Now who's going to cook? And poor Janelle. She's a wreck."

"Where is she?" Ryder pushed past Mike and Lance up the sidewalk to find his dear friend. He opened the bluebonnet-blue painted door at the far side of the wide front porch. Heather clasped the innkeeper's hands. Mike appeared at his side. "Take Heather upstairs. I need to speak with Janelle."

Mike sputtered.

He turned and lifted his brow. There was no time for arguing. Tank was accused of serious crimes that Ryder completely doubted he'd committed. But if he didn't get information and fast, not only would his friend be at risk, but who knew what the real murderer would do next.

As soon as Mike and Heather were gone, he crouched next to Janelle. "Tell me everything you know."

Janelle wiped her eyes and took two deep breaths. "Tank has been prepping for the wedding. One of the menu items, Jerk Chicken, he planned to do on the grill, along with the filets for the slider appetizer. He's an amazing chef, you know. Better than this town deserves."

Ryder nodded.

"Anyway, he filled all his propane tanks at the marina this weekend. Six or so, I think. They took the receipt when they were questioning him."

"What does the propane have to do with anything?" It was damn hard to set a building on fire with propane. Explosion, yes. Fire? No.

Janelle leaned toward Ryder and lowered her voice. "I over-heard Kessler telling Tank, when they were questioning him. He said whoever set the fire overrode the valve restriction on one of the canisters—one's missing—and pumped propane into the newspaper office."

"That doesn't make sense. The building would have to be airtight."

"That's what Tank said. They asked how he would know that." Janelle sniffed. "I mean really."

"Ventilation is the first rule of cooking," Ryder said as if he had any expertise in the field.

"Exactly. But the FBI man jumped on it as if Tank had confessed. Apparently, whoever did set the fire also stole some of the grease from the disposal bin. They doused the side of the building and left a trail away. That's how they were able to light the fire and not get blown up in the process. The missing propane canister was found in the neighbor's yard. Must have blown itself in there when the fire hit the gas."

The evidence pointed at the chef as if someone had deliber-ately put a neon sign flashing over his head. There were a lot of ways to torch a building, but this method was so convoluted. How had it even worked? Time to make a trip back to *The Peat*. But he had one more delicate question for the church-going woman. "What about an alibi?"

She looked away, and her already dark skin deepened a shade. "I don't know what you mean."

"Miss Janelle…"

"Ryder, he's innocent. This will all get cleared up. Besides, I know what you're asking, and I just can't…"

"It's not the sixties anymore."

"Not because he's white. Because we aren't married," she said, her voice barely above a whisper.

"And why is that? I know he's asked."

"You know no such thing." Janelle slapped at his arm. "I'm too old for him."

"He doesn't think so."

"Where would we live? My rooms here are tiny. His trailer needs so much more than a woman's touch. The man is a collector."

"If you're not careful, he's going to be living in a six-by-six cell." Ryder grabbed a pen from the cup on the doily-covered dresser that acted as the hotel check-in counter and wrote a phone number on the pad of sticky notes. "Call this man. He's the best criminal defense lawyer I know. He's in Houston. Tell him everything. I mean *everything*." Ryder gave her a pointed look. "And after this. Miss Janelle, say yes. Expand your rooms here or get a house."

Janelle picked up the pad. "I'll call."

Ryder went directly to the burned-out building that Mike could have died in. Everything pointed to Tank Murphy as the murderer and arsonist. Except it was so perfectly convincing, it smelled like a lie. There were better places to get rid of a body—the lake for one. And using propane and cooking grease to set a building on fire? That sounded like a reality show challenge. He could see the show writers seated around a table brainstorming: "What's the dumbest way to burn down a building?"

But why?

The back of the building was nearly destroyed. The space where Mike should have been sleeping that night. Whoever did this assumed she was there. Knew she lived there and which part of the building was her home. Didn't want to go inside. Mike might know the arsonist. Which meant it might be a local. Didn't rule out a conventioneer, but whoever had done this also went to a lot of trouble to set up Tank.

The firebug had drilled a hole through the base of the house, and the tubing had melted into it, right above the foundation. Based on the deep char marks, the grease had been poured along the base of the structure. Whoever it was knew propane was heavier than air. They'd concentrated the grease around the hole and run a trail back toward the fence line. So they were concerned about getting burned if they lit their experiment while standing too close. The propane was unpredictable, no guarantee what would happen when the spark of fire hit that hole. It had to have been done quickly.

The more he stared at the building, the more he suspected there'd been additional accelerant applied to the exterior. The arson investigators would report it, but nothing they would find would eliminate Tank Murphy as a suspect.

Only one place Ryder could get more information. He jogged back to his bike, made one quick call, and settled in for a long ride.

MIKE PACED AROUND the queen-sized poster bed in Heather's room. The call to Ryder went to voicemail again. Where was he? Ryder always answered her calls. If he thought she was going to wait in this room forever, he was mistaken. She dialed again.

Nothing.

Maybe he'd been in an accident. Acid rolled up from her stomach at the thought of him injured somewhere, his bike mangled. She called the sheriff's office.

"Daisy Sheriff. Deputy Silva. How can I help you?"

"Berta Ann. It's me, Mike. Have you seen Ryder? He's not answering. Has there been an accident?"

"Mike?"

"Yeah. I'm worried about Ryder."

"He went to Houston."

"What?" The statement was like a bucket of ice water dumped on her head. How did Berta Ann know where Ryder was and she didn't?

"Called about an hour ago. He's following up on something for Tank and wanted me to let him know if I hear anything. And to keep an eye on you."

Mike unclenched her jaw so she could speak. "Me? Why would you need to watch out for me?"

"Something about there still being a murderer on the loose who made an attempt on your life."

Fair point, maybe. But still. "How are you going to keep an eye on me when you're working?"

"Janelle was supposed to call if you left."

Oh my god. Mike finished her call with Berta Ann and nearly winged her phone out the second-story window. The man was infuriating. She didn't need a keeper. And she didn't need him to delegate his overprotectiveness. She glared at her phone.

Except that she *had* been calling around to find him, desperate for his advice about what to do for Heather. Her wedding was going to be a disaster, and it was all Mike's fault. She'd convinced Heather to have her wedding in Daisy, even acted as the coordinator. At the first sign of trouble, Mike had counted on Ryder to fix everything. So much for not becoming dependent on him.

Once she'd caved to weakness, as expected, he'd left her.

She still wasn't sure what to do, but whatever it was, she'd figure it out on her own.

CHAPTER SIXTEEN

Mike let herself into Ryder's shop. After spending the past few days with Heather, Mike's wardrobe was toast. Not that she had much left after the fire. But what remained, and the few items she'd picked up at T'weeds, needed to be washed.

Ryder's motorcycle and his truck were in the bays. No surprise. He'd sent a text when he got back from Houston. It sat on her phone still unanswered because she was still mad he left without telling her. She dropped the paper bag with her last few days of clothes on the washer then went to face the man she'd been avoiding. When she got to the apartment door at the top of the stairs, she hesitated. What was she going to say to him?

The door opened, and there he was in all his shirtless glory. Tousled hair, sleepy eyes, jeans unbuttoned… Sex personified. Mike's lungs froze. Would it really be so bad to move in with him?

Headline: Jinxed Journalist Caves to Alluring Alpha's Commands
Except what would she do when he left her?

"You coming in?" He raised an eyebrow with his question.

"I...uh...didn't want to wake you."

He grunted. "The bell sounded when you opened the door."

She stepped inside the apartment. "I need to wash my clothes."

"Be my guest." His lips pressed together, disappearing, and he shoved the door closed.

Shit. He hadn't tried to kiss her or touch her or anything. The word *guest* cut at her heart. "How was Houston?"

"Not as enlightening as I'd hoped."

"Sorry." The word came out automatically.

Ryder shrugged and wandered over to the kitchen. "Want some coffee?"

"In a minute. I'm going to start a load. Need anything washed?" Because dirty clothes were a safe topic.

"I'm good." He was. Incredibly good. She shouldn't be so resistant to moving in, but her gut told her it was a terrible idea. Her gut might be stupid.

Mike gathered her things from the corner of his small walk-in closet and went back down the stairs. The tension in the apartment followed her. They had so much to discuss—the murder, her office, where she was going to live, the wedding and if he would still be escorting her, assuming it still happened. Instead, they had retreated to laundry and coffee. After stripping off what she was wearing and adding soap, she slammed the machine shut, turned the dial, and pushed start. One of Ryder's spare shirts covered her as she marched back up, determined to have a real conversation with her boyfriend.

Coffee waited for her on the counter, exactly how she liked it. Ryder came out of the bedroom, pants buttoned and shirt tucked in, his sexy bare feet on display. She went to him and clasped her arms around his middle. A moment passed before he returned the gesture and kissed the top of her head.

"I'm sorry," she said into his cotton-covered chest. "Losing my home in the midst of this wedding is making me crazy. Not to mention finding a dead guy."

"Pulling away from me isn't going to make it easier."

"You left without even telling me." She didn't bother to disguise the hurt in her voice.

"You haven't exactly been responding to my attempts to communicate."

"I know." She craned her neck so she could meet his gaze. "Finding out who did all this might help get things settled."

Ryder smiled. "Your reporter skills haven't already solved the crime?"

She huffed and pressed back, but he didn't break his hold.

"Get your coffee." He released her. "I'll tell you everything I know so far."

They sat on opposite corners of the couch. Mow jumped into Mike's lap, pressing each paw like she was kneading dough until she curled into a relaxed ball. Mike envied the three-legged feline's agility. She scratched the sweet black cat's ears, waiting for Ryder to start first.

"I confirmed Chuck's dildo was used to kill Tony."

"Someone must have taken it at the demo. And if they do DNA analysis, they might find mine on it. I held it at the demo." She squeezed her shoulders forward to release the disgust from the realization she'd been holding the murder weapon.

Ryder nodded. "If they do, I'm not sure how long it would take to get results." He chugged some coffee. "I didn't get all my questions answered during the interrogation, but Tony's buddies said he was the one behind keeping the conference here. And someone had been calling him a lot before he died. Berta Ann's working on getting a phone dump."

"Could be a girlfriend."

"Possibly. Tony and Val were staying in the trailer Weenie owns at the marina, but I'm not sure how much time Val was spending there. Weenie said Frank met Val and her at the Pink Petals the night of the murder. He and Val left together."

"And since the murder, Val's been staying with her. But the night of the fire, Weenie was at her sister Olive's place."

"Why?" Ryder asked.

"Weenie's fighting to keep the conference here. She's afraid Val will move it. She made Olive talk to Albert and Kenny the night of the fire until they finally insisted they had to get back to the Bloom. Weenie wants Olive to run it."

"That seems unlikely."

Mike would have agreed if she hadn't spoken to the woman and heard it from her own mouth. "She's thinking about it. Weenie said Frank called about the fire when he was 'leaving her place,' but Frank and Val were fighting and I think they left the Petals separately, and Val made it sound like they needed to stay away from each other. I overheard them arguing when I went to the bathroom. Plus, I think 'her place' meant her house, not the trailer."

"Hmm." Ryder grunted. "I don't understand why anyone set the fire. What does hurting you or burning down *The Peat* gain the murderer?" A fierce scowl crossed Ryder's face. "Even though Tank has an alibi for both nights, I *do* know why he was arrested. Everything used to set the fire came from the Bay Leaves. But all of it was accessible from outside—the propane and the kitchen grease."

Mike's stomach growled. "Is it sick that talking about grease makes me hungry? Oh, and there's a new barbecue place. I went there with Heather, but we should go back."

"Where?"

She named the road, and he grunted.

"Not sure when it opened. Everything looked kind of new. No weeds in the gravel or anything. Traditional Texas style. It's called Junk's in the Trunk."

"Nice name." Ryder's mouth lifted at the corners briefly.

Mike ignored the flutter in her belly that had nothing to do with hunger. "What about Frank? I can't be certain it's him, but he admitted he was at the spanking demo. And he likes fire. He'd know how to set a fire with propane and grease."

"He was at the Petals that night."

"He could have set the fire and called it in. Weenie assumed he was at her place with Val. Maybe it's a fake alibi. Val was really upset after the fire demo. And I saw Frank at the barbecue place. With Kessler. Maybe Kessler thinks he did it too and was trying to question him? You know casual and stealthy, like I would."

Ryder's gaze bored into her. "I want you here tonight. It's making me crazy that someone who beat a man to death wants you dead and you're out partying with Heather. I can't sleep."

"But you went to Houston and left me."

"With everyone in town watching over you, including a sheriff's deputy."

Mike sipped her coffee and swallowed the urge to argue. "What were you even doing there?"

"A guy I know can do some deep background investigations. He doesn't like to talk over the phone. Kind of the paranoid type. But if you knew how to do what he does—the information that can be found on the internet—paranoia follows."

"Who are you having him check out?"

"A few people."

"Including the fire chief?"

"No jumping to conclusions and public accusations. I'm not saying you're wrong. I haven't eliminated him, but I'm not convinced he's the one either."

Heat crept up her cheeks, recalling the time last summer when she accused Olive of being the Stripper Killer. "I learned my lesson."

"Until I know who the threat is, I'd prefer you to stay here instead of with Heather. She can't protect you like I can."

"I don't want—" Mike's stomach growled, cutting off her words. Probably for the best. She didn't want to fight with Ryder.

"I'll make us something to eat." Ryder rose from the couch. Mow bounced off her lap to follow him.

"I'm going to check my clothes." And get some air because the apartment had shrunk in the last five minutes. The washer had finished, but a load of dry towels had been abandoned in the dryer. Mike pulled them out and started her small load. Then she took her time folding each towel perfectly and sorting them by size. Despite the fact she was hungry, she didn't want to have to tell Ryder that she hated his apartment. At least, she hated the idea of living there. Not that she had a lot of other options. Before she could decide how to have the honest conversation with Ryder, the bell for the garage rang. Someone was there, and she was stuck in the tiny laundry room in panties and Ryder's t-shirt.

Thumps down the metal stairs confirmed Ryder had heard the bell.

"Hey, Ryder."

Mike cringed. She'd left the door unlocked again.

"Letty?" Ryder sounded confused. "Have you seen—"

"I brought you something. I'm making the appetizers for a wedding rehearsal tomorrow, and I need my favorite taste tester to sample my wares." Letty tittered like a schoolgirl.

Mike peeked out between the open stairs. Letty held a plate of various items. The two Mike could see clearly were completely typical of the crackpot baker.

"Here." She held up what looked like a miniature dough twat to Ryder's lips. "It's a cheese puff, and I sliced it in half and tucked in a pepperoni with just a tiny piece of pimento."

To Mike's horror, Ryder parted his lips and allowed Letty to insert the pussy puff in his mouth. And then he moaned.

"That's good, Letty. What else you got?"

Seriously? He was going to encourage her?

Letty held up a narrow shot glass filled with opaque cream

and a red top. A miniature penis to go with her pussy puffs. Of course.

"Creamy cucumber soup shooter with a tomato cap."

Ryder took the shot.

Mike turned back to check on her clothes. Every minute she spent at the garage was one too many. The urge to swipe the folded towels to the ground was almost irresistible, but it would only make her look stupid. Ryder would never understand why Mike couldn't live there. She popped open the dryer and pulled out her mostly dry yoga pants. She wriggled into them, ignoring the still-damp seams. When she made her appearance from under the stairs, Letty was holding up something that looked like the shit emoji on a cracker, minus the googly eyes.

"Hey, Letty." Mike sauntered over to where Ryder stood with the flirty baker. "Whatcha got there?" Mike put a hand on Ryder's arm and reached for a cheese puff with the tiny pimento clit.

"Some samples for Heather's rehearsal cocktail party. Help yourself."

Mike smiled at her with her mouth full. The food always tasted better than it looked. The samples were no different.

"Good thing she didn't plan a rehearsal dinner, seeing as how Tank's been arrested. I told Janelle I could step in and do something with the ingredients to save the event."

Mike swallowed. "That's so nice of you. It might be difficult to work in the kitchen so close to where one of your former lovers was bludgeoned to death. I can't imagine."

Letty's mouth gaped momentarily. "I'm a professional. I can put emotions aside for the greater good."

"I'm so glad. I guess the last time you saw Tony was at the spanking demo. Did you get a chance to talk to him before Chuck had to kick him out for being intrusive with Berta Ann?"

"We didn't really speak. Our...*interaction* was long ago and very brief." Letty took a step back.

"Any idea whose *interaction* might not have ended so amicably?"

"None." Letty's jaw was tight.

"Guess it could have been anyone, seeing as how Tony went through women like a public restroom goes through toilet paper." Mike gave a half shrug and smiled.

Ryder cleared his throat. "Did you notice anyone at the demo acting oddly?"

Letty glared at Mike. "No more so than usual."

The dryer buzzed. "Excuse me," Mike said as she retreated behind the stairs and quickly folded the rest of her clothes, stuffing them into the brown paper bag. As she returned, Letty leaned into Ryder, whispering in his ear. Mike had to get out of there. "Thanks for the use of the machines," she called to Ryder as she practically ran past him. "I'll see you later."

"What about lunch?"

Mike slowed, turned back.

Letty popped another poop cracker into his pie hole.

Mike resumed her retreat and didn't stop until she was in her car. And then only long enough to toss her clothes to the passenger side and start it. Visits from people like Letty—anytime they felt like it because the garage was a business—were one of the reasons she couldn't move in with Ryder. No privacy. And no space. She was supposed to sit in the garage office and try to write? While people went in and out and he used pneumatic tools that hissed and burped all day long? Tears pricked her eyes, making the drive blurry.

She didn't fit in his life beyond the bedroom.

Back at the inn, she parked at the Bay Leaves restaurant. As she made her way around to the front, Fire Chief McCready came toward her. She glared at him as he neared her with a self-satisfied smile. Despite Ryder's warning about not accusing someone of murder like she had last summer, she opened her mouth and said, "I know what you did. You're not going to get away with it. Enjoy your freedom while it lasts, murderer."

"What?" He reached for her, but she dodged his grip.

Mike gripped her overflowing paper bag tighter and ran past him to the safety of the inn.

Janelle glanced up from the computer and narrowed her eyes at Mike. "You look like someone walked over your grave."

Still shaking, she asked, "Do you still have that little half room? Can I rent it for a month?"

CHAPTER SEVENTEEN

RYDER CHOKED DOWN THE MUSHROOM MOUSSE CRACKER. Delicious, but it was preventing him from calling Mike back. They were supposed to eat. He planned to cook, for fuck's sake. He swallowed. "Letty, everything's great, but I have to go."

"Do you think people will like it? The groom's family is used to city caterers, I'm sure. I want to show them we're just as good, even better than those fancy chefs."

"His family will be awed. Didn't you win a ribbon in the last county fair?"

"You know I did." Letty beamed. But she wasn't leaving.

Ryder set aside his Southern manners, took his friend's elbow, and guided her toward the exit as fast as she could teeter across the cement in her heels. "Heather is going to love what you created. You just caught me at a bad time."

"But Ryder, honey—"

He opened the door. The drive was empty except for Letty's red sports car. Mike's little beater was nowhere to be seen.

Shit.

"Are you sure you don't want one more taste?" Letty drawled and held out another cracker.

Ryder's stomach churned on what he'd already eaten. He'd been so close to convincing Mike to stay home. Letting him care for her. His phone chimed. "Sorry, Letty. Gotta go. But thanks. See you—" Ryder glanced at the screen. Janelle? He turned and went back in the garage, reading the text.

Janelle: *Ryder, Mike's here. She wants to rent the tiny room for a month. What's going on with you two?*

Before he could calm down enough to reply sensibly, his phone rang with his Houston contact. "Got info. Come tomorrow."

The call lasted less than three seconds. Trademark for the paranoid man.

His phone rang again. Damn. Give a guy one second to miss his girl.

"Collect call from FDC Houston. Will you accept the charges?" spoken by a digitized voice.

"Yes."

"Ryder, it's Tank. I just got back from court, and they issued bail. The lawyer you got me is supposed to call you, but I couldn't wait. Janelle okay?"

"No worries, man. She's fine. I told you I was taking care of things. How much is the bail?" Ryder winced when Tank answered. Unless she leveraged the inn, Janelle would never be able to come up with the collateral for that kind of bond, but Ryder could. And Tank was not the killer or the arsonist. "I got it covered. Pick you up tomorrow."

"I can catch the bus."

"I'm going to be in Houston anyway, and you've got a wedding to cater. Because if you're not back here, Letty is prepared to jump in, and my girlfriend will never speak to me again." Not that she would anyway.

The big Cajun man laughed into the phone, and the tension in Ryder's neck eased. "I'll be ready to cook up a feast never before seen. Your love life is safe."

Ryder wasn't sure food would fix his problems with Mike, but based on her metabolism, it couldn't hurt. As soon as he hung up, a voicemail notification chimed. He pulled up the message and put it on speaker.

"Ryder. Frank McCready here. Not sure what's going on with your girlfriend, but I don't like being accused of a crime I had nothing to do with. If she prints a word of this lie, I'll sue her, the town, and anyone else associated with the smear of my good name."

Fuck. Mike hadn't listened to a word he'd said. Pissing off the guy who might've killed someone and tried to kill her, no matter how slim the possibility, was a really bad idea. Ryder ran a hand through his hair and put his phone on the counter. The day was half gone, and he hadn't even taken a shower.

After steaming his brain clean and washing off the dust of travel, there was only one thing to do. Might as well return to Houston this afternoon and stay the night. Heather's fiancé Jason was supposed to arrive today in time for the rehearsal. Ryder was supposed to attend with Mike, but getting the chef back, getting info on the murder, and being back for the wedding was more important. Jason could take a turn keeping an eye on the women.

Ryder texted Mike: *Going to Houston again. Tank will be back in time to cater the wedding. Need anything, call Berta Ann.*

After a call to the deputy and caring for Mow's needs, Ryder rolled his truck out of the garage bay and settled in for the three-hour drive, four if he hit traffic. Either way, it left him plenty of time to come up with a way to fix things with Mike or figure out what he was going to do if he couldn't.

A weight settled on his heart. He'd been the happiest he could remember since meeting her. But maybe he just wasn't worthy of her. With his past and his ties to a side of life most people never wanted to acknowledge, much less see, he wasn't exactly happily ever after material. And maybe she'd figured that out.

MIKE DROPPED her paper bag of clothes on the single antique metal bed. It had been months since she'd stayed in the aerie, and it hadn't changed at all. Still cute and cozy. Still no place to really write. But it was hers for the next few weeks. She tucked her clothes away in the narrow tallboy and then went to find Heather to retrieve her laptop, her bridesmaid dress, and something to wear to the rehearsal. Maybe they could spend her last few hours as a single woman together before Jason arrived in town. But when Mike got to Heather's room, Jason was walking up the stairs toward her.

"Hey, Mike." Jason's smile lit up the hallway. "I made good time. How is she?"

Mike pasted on a bright smile that wasn't quite as genuine as his. "Happy. She'll be so glad you're here."

Before they could continue with small talk, Mike's phone buzzed. A text from Ryder. Leaving town again, but at least he had good news for Heather.

Heather squealed when she opened the door. "You're here." She clenched Jason in an encompassing hug, and Mike lingered in the hallway.

Maybe she should wait to get her things. But a deadline loomed. "Heather?" Mike got her friend's attention. "I just need to get my stuff. And can you loan me something for tonight?"

"Of course." Heather and Jason moved farther into the room and allowed Mike in.

"Ryder texted." Mike retrieved her clothes from the closet and slung her bag over her shoulder. "Tank's going to be here tomorrow to cook. The wedding will be perfect."

"Was there a problem?" Jason asked.

Heather gave Mike a slight shake of her head, eyes wide. Guess she hadn't shared the Daisy dramas with Jason.

"No. He had to stay overnight in Houston unexpectedly, and Heather was worried he wouldn't get back in time. But everything's fine." Not a lie, technically.

As soon as Heather added a simple cobalt-blue sheath to her pile, Mike escaped to return to room twenty-three. She had an hour before she had to dress for the rehearsal. With another article due, she should be writing, but focus on anything but Ryder eluded her. Before she'd found the body, her relationship with him had intensified beyond what she was ready for.

That wasn't quite true.

There were no red flags, and their passion was off the charts. He was the kindest, most protective, and supportive person she'd ever known. That included her brother, who had been amazing, but Ryder was even more. After the murder, and especially after the fire, Ryder had been clutching her so tight, and the temptation to melt into him, allow him to control everything, was huge. But if she did that, if she let him tuck her into the small spaces in his life, how would she grow? The last few months, she'd been more alive than the previous years of her life. More herself. More capable.

Hell, she'd helped catch a murderer last summer, and she could do it again. She opened her laptop and wrote down every fact she could, including the information Ryder had shared with her. As the words filled the page, details solidified. The holes became more obvious, and a nagging sensation that she was forgetting something important tugged at the back of her brain. She glanced at the time. Yikes. Less than thirty minutes before she had to be in the lobby to meet Heather. She slapped her laptop closed and raced to get herself together. First the wedding. Then the murder.

Mike drove to the church solo. Jason's SUV had been packed with Heather, his parents, and his best friend Ryan, the best man. The church lady appeared from nowhere as soon as they entered, wearing a flower-print dress, black flats, and pearls. She clapped her hands and then waved Mike over. "Let's line up and practice the procession."

Because walking slowly with an escort would be *so hard*. Although, since Mike was wearing a low heel, maybe she did need the practice. She slid her arm through the best man's and ignored the urge to retreat. Her body craved Ryder's touch, and no one else would do. Too bad her man had run off to the city again. She flashed a quick smile at Ryan and straightened her spine. Anything for Heather.

Forty-five minutes later, the church lady appeared satisfied that everyone in the wedding knew when to walk, pause, take flowers, and then walk back up the aisle. At least she wasn't demanding a sixth attempt. Hosting the rehearsal party at Pink Petals, the only bar within miles, suddenly seemed brilliant.

"Before you go—" the church lady called out.

Mike groaned.

"—I need just the bride and groom up here."

Mike slid into the nearest pew. Her escort went out the double doors into the still-warm evening.

The pastor appeared and spoke in low tones with Heather and Jason. Mike glanced around the church. Sunset streamed through the windows in the back, illuminating the wood pews in warm tones, completely different from the bright morning sun during the church service. Finally, Heather and Jason strode toward her, hand in hand, bringing Mike back to the present.

"Ready?" Heather asked.

Mike followed them out to the parking lot. The best man offered to ride with her so she wouldn't be alone. Mike suspected he wanted to get some space from the lovebirds and Jason's parents. He chattered away about the weather and the cocktail party. Mike missed Ryder's stoic silence. There was no space in the car for thought. Luckily, the town was small and the drive short.

Inside the Pink Petals club, Mike's jaw dropped. The club shimmered with romance. The stripper pole had been transformed into an architectural column, and copper fabric spoked out across the ceiling from it. The spotlights that lit the stage had been redirected to the seating area. The room glowed from pink gels, making all the guests look somehow younger and softer. Copper brocade tablecloths covered the cocktail tables. Jazz crooned from the sound system. Only the buffet tabled failed to ooze sophistication. Plates of slightly pornographic nibbles had been artfully displayed. Letty stood at one end in red cropped leggings and high-heel mules and an overly bright smile. Mike passed up the food, despite her hunger, crossed the imaginary state line to Louisiana, and went straight to the bar that hovered over the river. Before Caleb, who was acting as the bartender, could finish pouring her white wine, Heather appeared at her elbow.

"Isn't it beautiful?" Heather asked. "I'm so glad you talked me into having the wedding in Daisy. I know it's been a ton of work, but everything is just like I dreamed." Heather threw her arms around Mike. "Thank you."

Shimmery bubbles floated through Mike's middle. She'd managed to not ruin her best friend's wedding. "I'm so glad you're happy. Tomorrow is going to be perfect."

Heather turned to Caleb. "I'll have what she's having."

They clinked glasses as soon as he served Heather.

"Let's get a table near the stage. I promised Jason I'd dance with him."

"Isn't the groom supposed to hate dancing?" Mike replied as she followed Heather through the crowd who slowed their progress with congratulations and hugs for the bride. Mike ended up with Heather's glass and claimed the center table. Ryan joined her. Before Heather made it to the table, Jason led her up the stairs and into an easy traditional-hold dance. There was probably some official name for the dance or the style, but Mike had no idea what it would be. The song changed, but the rhythm remained slow and sweet.

"Care to dance?" Ryan asked.

No. She wanted Ryder. "I have no idea what I'm doing."

"Nothing fancy. I promise."

If Mike pouted all evening, her friend would be disappointed, so she followed him up the stairs. At least she didn't trip this time like the last time she'd been on that stage. She put her hand on her partner's shoulder and the other in his grasp. He placed his hand chastely on her waist. As he guided her back into the first step and around the stage as a few other couples, mostly older, joined them. Ryan was a good lead. Mike didn't have to think about her feet at all, but that left her free to catalog how unsatisfying it was to be in another's hold. Ryder should have stayed for the party. Could she blame him for leaving after walking out on him earlier and ignoring most of his texts the past week?

A lump formed in Mike's throat. What if he came back and didn't want her anymore? She'd been pulling away so hard, resisting moving in with him, resisting the closeness that had developed so quickly. What if he let her go?

Mike stumbled right as the song came to an end. She thanked Jason's friend and darted off the stage, ducking into the bathroom via the back stairs hidden behind a panel of fabric before anyone could see the tears running down her cheeks.

CHAPTER EIGHTEEN

RYDER RAPPED HIS KNUCKLES ON THE DARK SECURITY DOOR OF the nondescript ranch house. Footsteps approached, and Ryder made sure to face the screen directly. His connection wasn't above leaving Ryder on the porch if he didn't make himself recognizable. Several locks turned, dim light filtered through the tight steel screen, and finally it opened a scant inch. Ryder tugged the door open, rushed in, and closed it behind him. Xavier flipped all the locks back into place and peered at the surveillance camera feed for a few moments.

"Hey, X." Ryder spoke softly and without moving anything but his mouth.

Xavier turned from the video and peered at Ryder, his dark eyes wide and cataloguing. "Come."

Ryder followed Xavier through a dim hallway to a back bedroom lit only by computer monitors. Before they stepped in, Xavier pointed at a small table. Ryder placed his phone on it.

"Anything else? Fitbit? Apple watch?"

"Nah, man. I'm clean." Ryder wasn't about to wear a transmitter into X's house. Hell, he'd powered off his phone before he'd stepped foot on the property.

Ryder crossed into the secure room, and Xavier closed the metal door behind them, the magnetic lock sealing them in. The windows were blocked with steel-coated Styrofoam inserts. Probably decorated to look like shutters or curtains to any outside observers. Assuming anyone could see past the six-foot block wall with the white vinyl extension. Steel panels lay beneath the drywall all around the room. Ryder had helped install them when X bought the place. X controlled all of the transmissions in or out of the room, each fully encrypted behind untraceable IP addresses. It might seem like overkill to anyone who hadn't been in their line of work.

"Looked into the names you gave me: Tony Broussard, Albert Gaudraux, Kenny French, and Frank McCready. Frank's clean as a whistle, never been married, pays his taxes. If he's taking up killing or breaking the law in any way, it's a new hobby. He's a member of two BDSM clubs, one in Houston, one in Dallas. The date and time in question, his phone was at this address until 4:38 A.M. At *The Peat* at 4:45. Outgoing phone call to 9-1-1 at the same time. Then to this number at 4:47."

Edwina Alman.

"Albert, same deal. Although no club memberships. Aside from dressing up as an elephant, mostly at cons, he's currently employed as a project manager here." Xavier pointed at his screen to a commercial builder name. "And a former rig worker with this company." Xavier flashed a familiar logo.

Ryder gave a grunt of acknowledgement and waited.

"Where he met the other two, Kenny, born Kenneth, and Tony. They work at the same company Albert left. They're not quite as squeaky. Both have arrests in their youth. Tony had a DUI couple years ago, but the charge was dropped. Kenny has an ex-wife who's living well on half his salary. Tony was living better than his and his wife's salary combined could cover. Lot of cash transactions, if I had to guess."

"That's interesting."

"Kenny and Albert, if their phone GPS is accurate, were at a strip club here." X pointed to a map that showed the location of the Pink Petals. "And at 1:15 A.M. were here." He pointed to the Bloom with a View Inn.

Xavier was quiet for a minute, clicking through screens on his computer. "Found out what your girl's brother, David Mitchell, was working on." Xavier sat in a mesh ergonomic desk chair. His huge muscles filled the spaces between the padded arms.

With anyone else, Ryder would have prompted with a question. Instead, he waited.

"Heard of the INL?"

"Division of the State Department." Most people didn't know the State Department had an International Narcotics and Law Enforcement Affairs division. But Ryder already knew where David was working from his conversation with Ike.

"Right. Also your guy's official employer." X paused. "He spent time assigned to some European and Middle Eastern locations supporting a DEA effort to provide training."

Ryder leaned against the wall and crossed his legs. "What's the real story?"

"Not completely clear. The dots are there. No lines. He flew back to Houston about a year before his suicide on a same-day purchased commercial ticket. Haven't tracked down the why. Yet."

"Anything to do with his sister?" Maybe X had a missing piece that could help Ryder understand her resistance to their relationship.

"Negative. No arrests, hospitalizations, or financial issues. No requests filed by David."

For Ryder, the lack of documentation intrigued him more than if there had been a reason. If Mike's brother had been *his* op, he'd have generated something just to fill the gap, but not everyone had seen someone like Xavier work.

"Couple months later, Mr. Boy Scout is dating a stripper with a string of narcotics arrests." Xavier clicked the mouse, flicking through documents in a blur.

"Karla Bender."

"Deceased."

"Yep. I had an up close and personal of her body last summer."

X gave brief nod. "She'd been clocking a lot of miles when they started dating, and not on the pole. She was the weak link in a suspected narcotic smuggling ring. I unburied the last report Mitchell filed before he ate his gun. Had some sketchy details on how the loads were coming in by boat and then going all points by way of I-10, I-20, I-30, and eventually I-40."

Daisy was the transition point, or at least it had been last summer. What, if anything, did Mike's dead brother's report have to do with her office being burned down? Unless the ring suspected she knew something. But why, after so many months, would they act against her? "Anything newer pop?"

"Not yet."

"What's your gut say?"

"On the surface, they got an international dude, squeaky clean David, who's been doing corporate training, who suddenly goes undercover. Kind of sloppy work. Either in a hurry or a new guy coordinating. Stripper's dead. Agent David Mitchell's dead. Either there was more sloppy work I haven't found yet, or someone had an inside line."

The hair on Ryder's arms stood up. Insider threat was no joke. Gut instinct said to race back to Mike and put her under protective wraps. She'd hate him more for it—but fuck.

"Or David wasn't really doing training classes for remote offices and he had unique skills necessary to the op. Or he did something he shouldn't have while he was on assignment, and they moved him out and put him on a Podunk case they didn't really care about." X shrugged.

"Let me know if you find something more. Mike was supposed to have been at *The Peat*."

"Nearly got your girl?"

"Yeah." Ryder stood up from the wall. He had promises to keep, but after what he'd just learned, he had one more request. "Can I give you a couple more names?"

Xavier put his hands on the keyboard. "Go."

"Edwina Alman and Lance Kessler."

"I'll get back to you." Xavier escorted him out, and Ryder headed toward the detention center to pick up Tank. A call to the lawyer on the ride over confirmed the bond had been filed and Tank should be released soon. The lawyer was babysitting the process to make sure nothing got lost in the shuffle, like the chef. Two hours later, the big redheaded Cajun opened the door to Ryder's truck.

"You don't know how happy I am to see you, *bon ami*." Tank settled onto the bench seat and pulled the seat belt out fully before wrapping it around himself and clicking it in place.

Ryder started the engine. "No. It's me who's relieved to see you. I promised Mike you'd be back for the wedding."

"Have dey fig'erd out who really kilt dat rabid tiger?" Tank's normally subtle Cajun accent was thick with emotion, turned his THs into Ds, and chopped his words off.

Ryder had no trouble understanding what he said. "Not yet."

"Wasn't me." Tank grazed Ryder's forearm with his fingers. "I swear it."

"Not even a question."

"You put up the bail." Tank lifted his chin. "I'll pay you back."

"It's going to be returned as soon as the charges are dropped. And don't tell anyone I put the money up."

"You do this for all the folks in town, don't you?" Tank narrowed his eyes at Ryder.

"What do you mean?"

"This is why everyone's always giving you stuff. Never

understood why they treat you like the prince of Daisy. I mean, I know Janelle's always had a soft spot for you, but as an outsider, I didn't understand."

"Hardly an outsider. You've lived in Daisy for years."

Tank shook his head. "Getting arrested in my own restaurant—"

"It'll just be another town story after all this settles down and the real killer is caught." Ryder flicked on his blinker and merged into the traffic leaving Houston.

"If that ever happens."

"I'm not stopping until you're cleared. Only thing you gotta worry about is cooking up a feast."

"That I can do, my friend. That I can do." Tank leaned back and closed his eyes. In a few miles, he was snoring loud enough to make turning on the radio pointless. He probably hadn't slept at all the night before. Ryder let him rest while he tugged at the mystery of the murder, the problem with his girlfriend, and the info he'd acquired about her brother's death. The body count around Mike concerned him.

He rubbed at the tightness in his chest with his fist. How could he keep her safe when she seemed to want nothing to do with him?

MIKE DABBED under her eyes with dampened tissue, clearing the smears of mascara. What was with her and her emotions all over the place? Dancing with the best man shouldn't have made her ache so hard for her boyfriend. She shook off the stinging emptiness, practiced her smile in the mirror, and squared her shoulders.

Heather's rehearsal party music pealed through the bathroom when Mike opened the door. Her best friend was dancing with Jason and the rest of the wedding party. Even Heather's parents were on the stage moving their hips to a sexy pop song. Guess age didn't diminish desire.

At the table, Mike sipped from a glass of water and opened her phone. No texts. She typed a few messages, only to delete them, and finally went with: *At the Pink Petals with the wedding party. Miss you.*

After a few minutes of waiting, she tucked her phone away. Heather beckoned her on stage to a girls' anthem from the eighties. Yes, she did want to have fun.

After a million more songs, Mike slipped off the low heel and rubbed her toes. "My feet are killing me. No more."

Heather bounced down into the chair next to her. "Best rehearsal party ever."

"We should get you out of here. It'll be midnight soon, Cinderella."

"So what. My coach isn't a pumpkin." Heather grinned, tipsy with the beers she'd drank.

"Thought it was bad luck for the groom to see the bride on her wedding day?"

Heather turned toward Jason, who was chatting with some of his family and drinking from a water bottle. "Good point. Get me out of here."

Mike slipped on her shoe and grabbed her purse. Heather called out her goodbyes and blew kisses. They ran for the door and out to Mike's car, laughing the entire way.

As soon as they pulled out of the gravel lot, Mike asked the question that had been burning in her mind. "How did you know Jason was the one?"

A soft smile lit Heather's face. "He gets me. He hasn't tried to change me or improve me. Not even the stuff I do that I know drives him crazy."

"What could drive him crazy? You're perfect." Unlike Mike. But Ryder hadn't tried to fix her either.

Heather laughed. "You lived with me for two years. You know that's not true."

Mike shrugged. They'd been good roommates.

"Jason's easygoing."

Ryder could appear to be easygoing, but he really wasn't. He was in control.

"I'm so obsessive. He helps me chill."

"You? Obsessive? Never." Mike oozed sarcasm all over her uptight bestie. Maybe that was the thing that made their friendship work. Mike didn't obsess like Heather. Maybe relationships in general worked when there was a balance between the partners.

She pulled into the parking lot between Bay Leaves and the lake. Heather yawned as they made their way to the Bloom's wide front porch. Mike still hadn't sat in one of the idle rocking chairs with a book and a glass of lemonade. Maybe after the wedding. She'd have plenty of time since she was living here for the short term.

After leaving Heather in her room, Mike made her way to tiny room twenty-three and tucked herself into the single bed. She loved the peace and quiet of the space, but something was missing.

Ryder.

As much as she'd resisted, she needed Ryder. Wanted him. Loved him. She would compromise and make the garage work as her new home—if he hadn't changed his mind about her.

CHAPTER NINETEEN

RYDER TUGGED AT THE SLEEVES OF HIS SPORTS COAT AND SHIFTED on the pew. At least the weather had seen fit to comply with the perfect wedding plans. It had finally cooled off to pleasant instead of scorching. He checked his watch and glanced to the back of the church. The only person more anxious to see his girl than Ryder was the groom up front, waiting for his bride. At least Ryder hadn't had to put on a tie. Maybe he should have. Would Mike be disappointed?

The music started and saved him from his spiraling insecurities around his girlfriend. A couple slowly proceeded up the aisle. Followed shortly by another. Ryder sucked in a breath, and his heart pounded in his chest. Mike, his M, was at the back of the church, gorgeous in a pink dress that enhanced her subtle curves. A thin metallic layer on top made her every step hypnotic.

He tensed.

She was wearing heels.

No problem. He could get to her before she tripped. But somehow, she made it to the front, released from her escort. Ryder's hand curled, but then her sweet brown eyes met his gaze, a question lingering there. He tried to zing his approval to her through their connection. A gentle smile graced her lips.

He stood.

The bridal march started, preventing him from going to M but hid his gaffe of standing too early. As the bride passed, all Ryder saw was a moment in the future when he would be waiting at the front of a church, or wherever, for his bride, *his* M, to join him. His heart pounded under his compass tattoo, and he had no doubts about which direction he was headed. He committed to doing everything he could to make that future a possibility.

The service concluded quickly, and he filed out of the church with the rest of the guests. His conversation with Janelle from a few days earlier played on rewind as if he was giving himself the same advice: make room in his life for the person that mattered. Before he could second guess his decision, he retrieved his phone and dialed his favorite banker.

"Bradwell," the deep voice answered.

"Adam. Ryder. Sorry to call on a Saturday. Need your advice."

After getting the referral he'd called for, Ryder hung up, only to have his cell ring. Berta Ann.

"What's up?" he asked as soon as he answered.

"Got Tony's phone dump." The excitement in Berta Ann's voice was palpable.

"Find something?"

"Our sheriff stand-in?" Berta Ann paused. "He's in this thing up to his ass. Besides Albert, Kenny, and Val, there were a number of calls in and out to a single number. I called it from Chuck's phone. Kessler answered."

"Does he know it was you?"

She grimaced. "Not sure. I hung up right away."

"Where is he?"

"At the Bloom. Said he'd be providing extra security, what

with the possible killer out on bail, cooking for the reception. He didn't want anything happening to hurt the town's reputation."

Ryder set his jaw. How thoughtful of the lying bastard. Too bad Tony's phone record wasn't enough to prove anything.

"Where's Mike?"

"Pictures with the wedding party."

"You want me to head to the inn?" Berta Ann asked.

"First, can you contact Kessler's office? Get any info on how he got assigned here, who approved it. I have to get to the reception, so I'll keep an eye out. We can deal with Kessler after the party."

At the inn, Ryder checked in with Janelle. Busy with guests freshening up and last-minute details, she hadn't seen Officer Kessler. Ryder walked the outskirts of the property along the tree line, but nothing was out of place. He grabbed a glass of lemonade from the display under the tent and mingled with the other guests as he searched for his name on one of the place cards. Mike would be seated up front with the wedding party. If he wasn't close enough to keep an eye on her, he'd—perfect. Heather had seated him with a scant six feet between his chair and the bride's side of the head table.

As the wedding party arrived and the bride and groom were announced, Ryder kept his eyes open for a glimpse of Kessler. No sign. He chowed down on the probably excellent meal Tank served, but very little of it registered. Frequent eye contact from Mike kept him from hunting down the wayward lawman. She made a lovely toast to the newlyweds, funny and poignant, just like her.

Beyond the choreographed moves of the first dance, he caught a glimpse of a blond head moving around the outskirts of the tent. Why was Kessler really there?

Finally, Mike came to Ryder's table. "Ready to dance?"

"You just did. With another guy."

"Mandatory bridal party thing. Ryan's okay. But he's not you."

Ryder rose and gifted Ryan a killer glare. "Damn right." He took Mike in his arms and led her around the dance floor. "I need you to be alert. I got a new lead. Possibly the killer."

"Who?"

Ryder filled her in with whispered phrases as they moved to the music. "And I have no idea why he's here. But he's unlikely to do much in a crowd."

———

"Is HE AFTER ME?" Mike tripped over her feet, but Ryder kept her upright. "Do you think *he* set *The Peat* on fire?" And not Frank McCready? If so, that would be an awkward apology later.

"Not sure." Ryder's face blanked.

He likely suspected something, but that look said no way would she get any answers out of him. She closed the small gap between their bodies. She ached to leave the reception and fall into Ryder's bed. She'd missed him. He spun her, and Kessler shifted through her sightline momentarily. The late-afternoon sun glinted off his blond hair. She shivered.

"I got you."

He did, and Mike was grateful. But this was Heather's wedding, and Mike had promised to make it perfect for her bestie. "Holy shit."

"What?"

"Kessler was there, at the spanking demonstration." She stepped back, but Ryder tugged her closer, keeping her locked in the dancing embrace.

"Explain."

"I had my phone out to text you, and a guy knocked into me. Putting on his cheetah head for his costume. The light caught his hair, but I didn't really see his face. Just enough to know I didn't know him. Then at the church. Something was bothering me. He told us he got to town the morning I found Tony."

"He lied," Ryder said flatly.

"That doesn't make him the killer."

"It gave him the opportunity to grab the weapon. And be in the right place to commit the crime. He acted like he didn't know Tony, or Albert or Kenny for that matter. He's a furry, living near Daisy. He had to know them previously. Not to mention all those phone calls."

"It doesn't make sense. Why would Tony and Lance be calling each other about the conference?"

"I don't think that's what they were talking about."

Before Mike could ask her next question, Heather tapped her shoulder. "Where's the cake?"

Mike glanced over to the round table in the corner of the tent to the right of the head table. *Shit.* "Um. On the way. Last-minute frosting issue. No worries."

Heather nodded. "I need to pee desperately. You gotta help me hold this dress."

"I told you not to get such a poofy dress." Mike sighed. "Go. I'll meet you at your room. I just gotta tell Ryder one thing."

Heather made her way through the crowd, pausing to acknowledge people. When she was finally out of ear shot, Mike pulled her phone from her dress where she'd tucked it in the side of her bra. "Can you *please* find out where the cake is? I'll distract Heather. I'm gonna kill that baker if—"

"On it."

She opened her contacts list and dialed for him.

Ryder took her phone. "Keep your eyes open."

After wrangling yards of white frothy fabric, Mike could have used a drink. Too bad the party didn't have any liquor. "You should touch up your lipstick."

Heather's hand flew to her mouth. "Really?"

Mike nodded, praying Ryder had magically made the cake appear. Heather spent far longer touching up her makeup than Mike expected. Thank goodness.

"Am I okay?" Heather asked.

"Perfect." Mike only felt a little guilty about managing her friend. Heather went out into the hallway first, and Mike pulled the hotel room door closed. She flinched at the high-pitched yelp. *Damnit.*

Did she close the damn dress in the doorway?

No.

She turned.

Oh *shit*. Mike blinked at the situation in front of her like it would go away if she wished hard enough.

Lance Kessler. And he had a choke hold on her best friend. Heather's eyes were wide with terror.

Headline: Cold-Blooded Killer Captures Bestie Bride

No one was in the hall. Likely no one was in the hotel.

"Don't scream."

"Duh." Mike bit the inside of her cheek. Not the way to play this. His hand connected with her face, and pain exploded, leaking out of her eyes. "What the hell?"

"Not one fucking word, Mitchell. I know your boyfriend has me fingered for the murder."

Mike bit back the argument that Ryder was likely more pissed about him burning down her home than killing Tony. If she could get him talking, he might get distracted.

"Let's go. And you better just shut up and follow, or I'll snap your friend's neck like a fucking chicken." He patted his holstered gun. "Then I'll take you down before you get ten feet." He led them down the long hall to a narrow, steep emergency stairway, probably from when the Victorian was originally constructed.

"This is ridiculous. Why are you kidnapping Heather and me?"

"She's just in the way." He shook the bride like a rag doll. "But you... You saw me at the demo. You're the only one who can put me in Daisy. Then you started asking all those questions. Getting Ryder involved. Demanding he help you 'find the killer.' And you recognized me at the inn."

"Not from the demo. I didn't even see your face." But his face was familiar. Where? *Think, Mitchell. Think.*

Kessler shoved Heather down the first stair. Her friend grappled with her dress, trying to lift it. Mike glanced down the hall. No one. She could run, but she might get shot, and she couldn't leave her friend at his mercy. She followed, clinging to the tiny round railing with one hand and bracing against the wall with the other. How did women wear heels every day, and why? She was going to break her neck.

"Move," Lance barked back at her.

"Why'd you kill Tony?" Short and obvious, but maybe he'd answer.

"Self-defense. That asshole attacked me. Called me to meet him for a threesome with some chick who wanted to yiff. Total fucking liar."

"You lied about getting into town that morning." And he was probably lying about Tony attacking him. "How did you even know Tony?" Her heel slipped out of her shoe. Could she use it as a weapon? Not with any certainty of taking him out. She slid her foot back in and took the next stair. Heather continued to struggle, unable to look down at the stairs with Lance's hand on her neck and the pool of fabric around her legs.

"I've known that bastard forever." Lance yanked Mike's arm. "Stop with the questions and keep moving. You know, you're a lousy reporter. If I'd known how bad you suck at your job, I might not have torched your place."

Ouch. That wasn't necessary. He was already ruining Heather's wedding. "I'm a better reporter than you are a cop."

"Shut up and move." He shoved Heather again.

Her dress caught. Five steps before the bottom. The sudden stop jerked Lance off his perch. He dropped to the floor below, landing on his knees.

"*Run*," Mike yelled at Heather, who yanked the fabric free with a rip and gazelled over Kessler, bursting through the back door with a curdling scream. Mike tried to leap over Lance, but he grabbed her ankle and she crashed. Damn those heels. Before she could yank one off and clobber him like she should have done earlier, he was dragging her to the parking lot.

Heather, white dress glowing in the dusky evening, bolted across the grass, ripped fabric flowing behind her, arms waving, still screaming like a banshee. The guests, eerily lit with the yellow glow from the strands of Edison lights, turned in mass and froze, almost like a horde of zombies. Kind of perfect for an October wedding.

Mike cursed how her brain worked. A killer was dragging her god knew where, and she was capturing mental images and drafting headlines for her blog.

The Bay Leaves lot was packed with cars. A van stood open, idling. *Shit.* Did Kessler have an accomplice? Bad things happened in vans. She slowed her already mincing steps. He yanked her arm.

"Move," Kessler hissed.

Oh, sure. Let me hurry toward my untimely death.

A woman stepped out of the wide van door and popped open a tea cart. She slid Heather's perfect cake onto the top. Three tiers, ivory buttercream frosting, fall-colored fondant leaves accenting the yellow and orange frosting chrysanthemums on each layer. The antique bride and groom posed on top in a clinch. Columns and a tray supported the top layer, hovering over the bottom two. Exactly what they'd ordered and a brilliant solution to the weighty topper problem.

"Help!" Mike wrenched out of Kessler's hold.

The woman turned. Kessler bolted. Footsteps and hollering

filled the air behind Mike. The entire male guest list and some of the women raced toward her.

Mike snatched up the top tier of the cake and launched it at Kessler like it was a half-court money shot in a game of hoops. The heavy topper connected perfectly with his temple, cake and frosting splattering across his face. He stumbled, dropping to the gravel-covered ground.

Berta Ann bolted past Mike as Ryder lifted her into his arms. Berta Ann dropped a knee onto Kessler's back and smacked her cuffs on his wrists. She yanked him upright, and he weaved, shaking his head like a dog to clear his eyes.

"Nice shot, M," Ryder growled in her ear. He squeezed her so tight, she could barely breath. "You scared the shit out of me."

"I'm okay." She dropped her head to his shoulder.

Home. He was her home.

"I'm taking him in." Berta Ann tugged the disgraced officer toward her patrol car. "I'll call his office for backup."

Ryder nodded once.

"Mike." Heather carefully brushed the hair away from Mike's face with the hand her new husband wasn't holding. "Are you okay? How's your cheek?"

"I'll be fine." She wiggled in Ryder's arms. Ryder lowered her to the ground but kept his arm around her. "I'm so sorry about your cake, your dress, and your wedding." Jason's family heirloom was still in one piece—mostly. "The cake was beautiful, and you didn't even get a picture."

Heather laughed. "Are you kidding me? This is gonna make an epic story. One we'll tell the grandkids."

Jason retrieved the treasured figurine, his eyebrows at his hairline. "Grandkids?"

"Of course. I'm not letting you go ever." Heather kissed Jason, who scooped her up, just like the bride she was.

"Better get started on that plan now," Jason said before he stalked off toward the hotel. The sun setting on the marina

HELL HATH NO FURRY

created the perfect picture. Heather waved, a huge smile on her face.

"We should get some ice on your cheek." Ryder led her inside the restaurant and tied up a baggie of ice. He followed her up the narrow stairs. She should have felt nervous being back where Kessler had assaulted her, but with Ryder at her back, she was nothing but safe. They got to her room, and she opened the door.

"Unlocked?"

"This dress doesn't have pockets."

Ryder closed his eyes and shook his head. He went in before her, checked the bathroom and under the bed. Really, the room was so tiny, it was kind of ridiculous. If someone was in there, they would have heard the person breathing, but she didn't say anything. She kind of liked his protective side.

He pressed the ice to her cheek gently. "Please stop scaring me to death."

"Didn't intend to."

He took the bag away, lowered his lips to hers. The connection lit, not with an explosion, but with a warmth, like a sunrise. A sense of love washed over her like ocean waves. Deeper and deeper. She wasn't drowning, she was floating, cradled in his love, warmed by his heart. She moaned and tugged him to the bed.

He released her. "Keep this on your cheek." The ice pack against her face. "And keep this door locked."

"Wait. Where are you going?"

"To help Berta Ann with Kessler."

"I should come too. I can change in a minute." Mike kicked off her dreaded heals and glanced around the tiny room for a pair of jeans.

"You'd have to sit in the lobby for I don't know how long. It's better if you stay here."

"But—"

"Berta Ann will want to interview you and Heather. Don't worry, I'll tell you everything I find out afterward." He carefully tucked a tendril of hair behind her ear. "You were amazing today." He lifted her hand clutched around the ice pack and pressed it to her cheek. "Be back as soon as I can." Then he was gone.

CHAPTER TWENTY

MIKE'S FINGERS FLOWED OVER THE KEYBOARD, TYPING UP THE crazy Daisy wedding reception from the previous day. It might not be appropriate for *The Daily Peat* site, but she could share it with Heather when she got back from her honeymoon. A story for her grandchildren. Her cell chimed.

"Hey, Mike. We're leaving."

"I'll be right down."

She shoved her laptop off her legs to rest on the bed, slipped on her blue flats, and raced down the front stairs.

Heather and Jason stood on the porch with their packed bags beside them.

Mike propped her hands on her hips, giving the new Mrs. Reinhardt the stink eye. "I can't believe you're leaving without tasting Tank's stuffed French toast. It's unbelievable."

"Mike." Her bestie wrapped her in a hug. "I'm so sorry, but if we don't go now, we'll miss our flight. You know how bad I want to see Hawaii."

"Fine. But that toast is way better than a tropical honeymoon." Okay, it was probably a distant second, but Mike was hungry.

"Rain check. When we get back, I'll come up for a girls' weekend. No weddings, no appointments, and hopefully, no dead bodies."

"Deal."

Heather and Jason sped off toward his car. She'd be back. She had to be—her car was being stored in Ryder's garage until they came home. Mike clung to that fact like a kid with a favorite stuffy, already missing their tight friendship. Her bestie was married and leaving. Not dead, but definitely not going to be the same. Technically, Mike had left first, living in Daisy, but she could have moved back to Houston at any time.

No, that was a lie.

There was no way she would ever be happy living in Houston if Ryder remained in Daisy. Speak of the devil, a movement up the walk caught her eye. Ryder strolled toward her with that signature sexy gait—powerful legs wrapped in denim, white t-shirt tucked in, long dark hair loose. Mike's entire body lit, and her heart crashed against her breastbone. She had some apologizing to do for the way she'd been acting for the past month. If she had to adjust to living at the garage to make their relationship work, then she would find a way. Somehow. If he still wanted her there.

"M."

One fucking letter, and her panties caught on fire. "Hi."

"Take a drive with me?" Ryder held out his hand to her. "I got doughnuts."

"I would have said yes without." She placed her hand in his and beamed him a smile. "Coffee?"

"Of course."

In the truck, as Ryder drove, Mike licked the icing from her fingers. Letty's maple bars, with their bonus doughnut holes, might look like a cock and balls but they were delicious. Ryder had been driving all over while they ate, telling her stories from when he was a kid living in Daisy. Where Donny had crashed his bike, needing ten stitches. Where they'd tried to catch a cat to keep as a pet and nearly been shot with rock salt for trespassing in Old Man Johnson's backyard. Learning to swim in the lake. Mike enjoyed hearing about his childhood, but that was not the conversation she craved.

"What about Kessler?" she finally asked.

"He hired a lawyer, and he's swearing self-defense."

"Seriously? Sure wasn't self-defense when he attacked me and Heather." Her cheek was purple. Not exactly an accident. And Berta Ann had taken pictures when she'd come to the inn to do the formal interview. Even if Kessler got away with the killing, she could file assault and battery charges against him.

"He says that Tony took the dildo and arranged the meeting. That Tony attacked him. And that he went overboard in defending himself, so he didn't think anyone would believe him."

Mike snorted. "That's 'cause he's a liar."

"And he's trying to pin the arson on Frank—"

"He admitted he torched *The Peat* to Heather and me."

"Since he was driving Donny's patrol car and it's the property of Daisy, Berta Ann searched it and found a huge grease spot in the trunk that wasn't there when he was issued the keys. Berta Ann had the damn thing detailed for the asshole."

"I bet he's regretting her Southern hospitality about now," Mike said.

"He might be regretting a lot of things. Berta Ann's got CSU trying to match it to the Bay Leaves grease bin contents. And she found out he's had arson investigation training in the military. Apparently he thought he learned more than he really did."

Mike laughed, but even she heard the bitter undertone. She missed *The Peat*.

"He also didn't have a good explanation for all the phone calls with Tony. They went to high school together. Lance claims Tony was trying to talk him into starting a new adults-only furry convention. I'm not buying it. Especially after he showed me his contact list to try to prove he didn't know Albert or Kenny. You'll never guess whose numbers he did have."

"Who?"

"CK and Karla."

The two names from last summer that could make Mike's blood run cold. One dead, and the other never to set foot in Daisy again. Thank God.

"He's claiming to know them from earlier conventions. But he has no other convention contacts in his phone."

"What about…" Mike bit her lip. "What about my brother? Was he in the contacts?"

Ryder picked up her hand from the bench seat. "Not that I could tell. The feds are going to be taking over the investigation and prosecution. I don't know exactly what will come out, but my gut says this is tied in some way to the drug running that was happening through the Pink Petals last summer. Olive's locked out that avenue of distribution."

"This is what my brother was investigating?"

"I'm pretty sure he was undercover in this organization—or trying to be through Karla. I've got a very talented contact looking into more information on Kessler and some others because I'm starting to agree with you that he didn't kill himself."

Mike sucked back a sob. "I *know* he didn't."

"We don't have the whole picture yet."

"Picture!" All the pieces clicked into place, including what she thought she'd forgotten.. "I know why he set *The Peat* on fire. The picture. He was in the picture with David. He knew my brother."

Ryder pulled into the driveway of a Tudor-style faux mansion with a For Sale sign. "Let me call Berta Ann right now." He turned off the truck. "She'll be able to track down the records, and she's searching Donny's house for anything Lance might have left there. He can claim self-defense all he likes, but we will get to the truth."

Ryder's conversation with Berta Ann was brief. "She'll get the information to the feds. He won't get away with what he did."

Mike should have felt relief, but grief still weighed heavy on her heart. When Ryder didn't start the truck, she glanced around. "Why are we here?"

They were in Weenie's ritzy neighborhood on the outskirts of Daisy, near where the river flowed into the reservoir to make the lake. He released his seat belt and shifted on the bench.

"I heard you."

"About my brother?"

"About everything. About how there's no room at the garage for you. How you need certain things, like space and privacy, to be happy." He lifted the half-empty doughnut box and placed it on the dashboard. He held his arms open. "Come here."

Mike freed herself from the seat belt and slid into his embrace, letting his warmth ease the sting of talking about her brother. "I could make the garage work."

"You don't have to fit in the corners of my life. I don't want you to make yourself small to be with me. I want you to be able to settle in and grow. To be the amazing woman you are. So, I was thinking, maybe we could look for a place where we both fit. Somewhere near Daisy, because I just can't leave it."

That explained all the childhood memories. "I don't want you to."

"I'll keep the garage."

A car pulled up next to them in the driveway. A polished-looking woman with bleached, hot-rollered hair and a magenta skirt-suit emerged from the shiny black SUV.

"I asked a Realtor to show us some places."

"On a Sunday?"

"We don't have to decide on anything today. We're just looking. But would you be willing to consider staying in Daisy, with me?"

Mike's chest nearly burst with the surge of love. "You'd do that for me? Buy a house?"

His chin dropped to her shoulder. "I'd leave Daisy, if I have to."

"No. I love it here, too."

A noise rumbled out of Ryder somewhere between a grunt and a roar. "Thank God, because I dreaded having to move to Houston. Be like having my soul ripped in half. Worth it to be with you, but—"

Mike put her fingers on the lips of the man who barely spoke. She tilted her head back and met his intense gaze. "I'm staying."

Ryder pressed his lips to hers. The kiss over far too quickly. "Good. Let's go look at this house."

"I'll look at this place. But we're not moving into this ridiculous monstrosity."

"It's got a basement." Ryder's voice was low and filled with promise.

A tingle of interest in his intentions for such a space zinged up Mike's spine.

"Room for a cross or a pole..."

Heat flooded Mike's cheeks. "We should talk about why you might want all that, but not while the Realtor is waiting."

Ryder raised an eyebrow and gave a sexy half grin. "Come on, naughty girl. Let's go shop for a home."

CHAPTER TWENTY-ONE

MIKE'S CELL RANG WITH AN INCOMING CALL. SHE FREED HERSELF from Ryder's embrace and swiped it up from the nightstand. Heather. "Oh my god. Are you calling me from Hawaii?"

"We just finished a late lunch." Heather's voice was so familiar but different. Happier, but with another quality Mike couldn't quite name. "We're going snorkeling later and taking a helicopter ride tomorrow."

"That sounds amazing."

"It has been. It's so pretty here. So much cooler than Texas, but it rains a lot."

"Great reason to stay inside." Mike loaded her tone with innuendo.

"We've done plenty of that." Heather laughed. "How are you and Ryder?"

"Good." Mike glanced at the naked man laid out beside her.

"We're gonna be home in two days. I need to get my car. Where should I meet you? The inn?" Heather was fishing.

"No. Just call me. Ryder and I can take your car to Houston. The four of us can have dinner, and you can tell me all about the honeymoon."

"Did you guys finally work everything out?" Heather huffed.

Mike laughed. "Yes. I'll tell you all about it when I see you. Go enjoy your honeymoon."

"Tell her about what?" Ryder rolled over and took Mike's quiet phone from her hand. He checked the screen and put it facedown on the nightstand, shifting over her naked body completely. His hard cock pressed into her belly. "What are you telling Heather?"

"All our secrets." She grinned up at him and swiveled her hips.

He gripped her wrist, lifting it over her head. "I might have to punish you for that."

"Promise?"

Both wrists ringed in his grip, he raised an eyebrow and grunted. Mike's pussy turned to lava as Ryder tied her hands to the headboard.

He nuzzled her neck and nipped at her collarbone before slowly sliding lower. His tongue on her breast had her arching into his mouth, silently begging for more. Saying it out loud would only lead to him slowing down. He was perverse that way. She bit her lip and savored every teasing lick across her beaded breasts, along the sensitive undersides. Her boobs weren't very big, but he sure found ways to enjoy them.

He sucked one of her nipples into his mouth and hummed. The vibrations traveled through her belly and right into her clit. "Please, Ryder."

"Begging already."

"God yes. I need you inside me."

"Pretty sure I spent most of the night inside you."

"More. Again."

He slid a finger along her pussy. "So wet for me already."

She panted her agreement. If he would only put his fingers inside. Give her some relief. He swirled the wetness along her puffy lips, down lower, around her sensitive pucker. She bucked her hips at the forbidden sensation. He teased her hole again as his mouth trailed down. He tongued her clit, his finger still teasing her back entrance.

Mike was torn between arching away from him and opening wide. He licked her deep and slow. Wide it was. She dropped her knees to the sides, lifting her pelvis to his magic mouth.

"So hungry." His voice was a growl.

"Starving for you. Always."

"Me, too." He buried his face between her legs and feasted until she exploded for him. "That's one."

"If this is your idea of punishment, I plan to be very naughty all the time."

Ryder laughed so hard, his hair flew back. "M, we're just getting started."

"Oh shit."

A speck of evil tinged his stare as he rose. "I'll be right back."

The satisfaction of her first orgasm wore off before he returned, and her efforts to slake her growing thirst for him failed. He had two items in his hands. The first, a red feathered wand. The second... "Are you serious?"

"You can tell me no."

She bit her lip and considered. If she hated it, he'd take it out. She didn't doubt for a second that while she appeared to be at his mercy, one word would end their play. He had all the control she granted him.

"M?"

"Okay. I trust you."

He locked his eyes to hers. "I'll never give you a reason not to, M."

Tears pricked her eyes. Of course he wouldn't. He was Ryder.

He set the wand to the side, opened the nightstand drawer, and took out two condoms and lube. He slicked up the skinny butt plug. "Ready?"

"As I'll ever be."

His focus intensified, sending tingles zipping out to her knees and up to her belly button. He hadn't touched her with the toy, and she was already on fire and gushing wet. The cold surprised her when he pressed the tip to her ass and made a small circle. She squeaked.

"Good?" He circled the toy again with more pressure.

"Damn." She nodded, lifting her head trying to see what he was doing to her body to make her feel like that. Pressure. She dropped her head. Was she really going to let him plug her ass? Stretching, a little sting. She sucked in a breath.

"Still good?"

"Uh-huh." What were words?

More stretching. Full. Her ass closed over the neck of the toy, clutching the body inside her. "Oh."

Ryder gave her a devilish grin, his eyes sparkling. He twisted the toy with a gentle tug, and everything below her belly button lit up.

"Too much." She could come just from him teasing her.

He chuckled. "Just getting started."

The feathers of the wand drifted across her inner thigh, one after the other with the barest of contact. When had Ryder picked up the wand? The feathery sensation traveled behind her knee and across the bottom of her foot. She clenched her ass. The toy shifted deeper, felt bigger. "Oh fuck."

"Not yet." He dragged the wand along the bottom of her other foot. The more she squirmed, the more intense the plug in her ass became. He toured her body like a back roads trip, mapping every sensitive spot on her pelvis, across her mound, up her stomach, along her sides, around her breasts. Each new place raising the need growing between her thighs. He circled the tip of each breast.

"Ryder." It was a plea, a threat, a prayer.

He dropped the wand and slid a condom over his thick cock.

It bobbed as he positioned himself over her, lifting her legs up and open. His gaze locked to her ass and smiled. "This is going to feel so fucking good, M."

"Now," Mike insisted. He could stop with his teasing and just fuck her already.

He tilted his hips and pressed his cock into her pussy with one long, slow, stretching thrust. His cock was three times bigger than normal, or might as well have been with that plug taking up so much space. He filled her, every space of her. Between her cells, there was Ryder. Even her brain was full with him. His gaze locked on her, his warm dark eyes like liquid chocolate coating her in him.

Against every resistant, independent, don't-rely-on-others streak in her, she loved it. Craved it. Craved him. Just him.

With a shift of his hips, he started a rhythm of movement that pounded through her like a heartbeat. Every shift shattered her a little bit more, reconstructing her into the image of who she'd always wanted to be.

She clenched around his cock, the plug nudging deeper. He moaned. The sound vibrated through her chest, pushing her over the edge and into an abyss where her body shivered and quaked. Clenched against him. And then he fell in with her, his hips losing their pace, jerking in a wild, unpredictable frenzy as they came. His hair curtained around them, and his eyes poured love into her.

Minutes or months later, he fell to the side, panting. "Give me a sec."

"Free me. I have to touch you."

He rolled and released the ties at her wrists. She twisted into his body, molding herself to him. She drifted off, only be awakened by Ryder liberating himself from her embrace. "Don't go."

"Let me clean us up." He disappeared into the bathroom for a few minutes before returning, still naked, with a cloth in one hand. "Gotta get that plug out of you."

Until he said the word, she'd forgotten about it. Once he'd retrieved it, she felt empty. She curled over, and he covered her up. "Be right back."

He jostled her awake, tugging her into his arms.

"I love you, Ryder." She hadn't intended to tell him, especially not right after sex, but she didn't regret sharing the truth.

"I've been in love with you for months."

"You love me?" Her heart stretched to hold the revelation.

"Since practically the first moment I met you this summer."

"Liar. You didn't want me on your bike." Especially after she got road snot, that tar-based goo, on the brand-new seat.

"But then you showed me your hook shot."

"Why didn't you say?"

"Didn't want to scare you away."

She pressed a kiss to his lips. "Not going anywhere. Ever."

AUTHOR NOTE

Thank you for reading Hell Hath No Furry, Book 2 in the Dirty Daisy Mystery series. Writing in the world of Daisy, TX is one of my guilty pleasures and I'm glad you joined me for the ride.

I would love, love, love for you to leave a review somewhere about this book. As you may have guessed, Daisy can't be found on a map, so your review may be the only sign post another reader has to find this crazy town.

Also, if you liked this book you might like my others. I send a monthly newsletter and subscribers get a free prequel to my Melting Hearts series. You can subscribe on my website: jordynkross.com

ACKNOWLEDGMENTS

First, last, and always, thank you to my husband for supporting my writing in every way. I love you!

Thank you to my Reines for everything you do!

Thank you to Brandi Doane McCann for another amazing cover.

Thank you to Jenny Rarden for the fantastic editing.

Thank you to my amazing beta readers who made this book infinitely better.

Thank you to Passionate Ink for providing a safe and educational forum for erotic romance authors.

And thank you to my readers who make writing worth all the struggles!

ABOUT THE AUTHOR

Award-winning, best-selling author, Jordyn Kross, is an unapologetically naughty novelist who spent years honing her writing skills with tech manuals and marginal poetry before finding her passion for writing sexy, boundary-stretching happily-ever-afters.

When she's not writing, she's attempting to garden in the desert Southwest, hiking with her insane pound posse, and admiring that handsome man wandering around her house who continues to stay.

Jordyn enjoys saucy double entendres, pretending to be an extrovert, and is well-known for having no filter. And when she's not in social media jail, she can be found on Facebook, Instagram, and BookBub, or hiding in a dark cave peering out at the X file formerly knows as Twitter.

www.ingramcontent.com/pod-product-compliance
Lightning Source LLC
Chambersburg PA
CBHW030939210726
48290CB00007B/2250